Chelsea's smile vanished, and her cheeks went pale.

"Chels?" Buck asked with alarm.

She turned the paper over and held it up toward the dim streetlamp light for him to read.

Buck's blood steamed in his veins. It was a picture of her, taken outside this very bar probably as she'd headed in to work earlier this evening. Someone had scribbled a message over it. The rain had smeared the ink, but the threat was clear.

Stop what you're doing—or someone will get hurt.

"I don't know what that means. Stop what? Who's he going to hurt?"

Buck glimpsed a tiny flare of light from the alleyway across the street and reacted instinctively. By the time he heard the pops of a gun being fired, he'd dragged Chelsea up against his chest and twisted her away from the shots. He dove for the pavement a split second before her windshield exploded...

To 2021. You threw a lot of challenges at me while I was writing this book, and it really impacted my ability to create and be productive for a while. A cancer scare. Surgical procedures. Downsizing and moving my mom after fifty years in the same big house. Hubby in hospital. Mother in hospital. Father-in-law in hospital. A break-in and financial challenges. But I survived. I got through it all. Through God's grace, a little cursing, some despair and, ultimately, stubborn perseverance, we all got through it. We're managing. I learned a few lessons and I'm writing again. Check in with your doctor once a year. Hug your loved ones. Have faith in something greater than yourself. Be kind to yourself and to others. Ask for help when you need it and say thank you. Thank you to my editor, agent and publisher for giving me the time I needed to take care of myself and my family. Thank you to my readers for your patience and support.

To 2022. I'm back. I've got a lot of hope for you, baby!

DECODING
THE TRUTH

USA TODAY Bestselling Author

JULIE MILLER

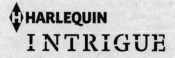

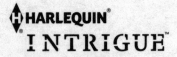

ISBN-13: 978-1-335-58230-0

Decoding the Truth

Copyright © 2022 by Julie Miller

Harlequin Enterprises ULC
22 Adelaide St. West, 41st Floor
Toronto, Ontario M5H 4E3, Canada
www.Harlequin.com

Printed in U.S.A.

Julie Miller is an award-winning *USA TODAY* bestselling author of breathtaking romantic suspense—with a National Readers' Choice Award and a Daphne du Maurier Award, among other prizes. She has also earned an *RT Book Reviews* Career Achievement Award. For a complete list of her books, monthly newsletter and more, go to juliemiller.org.

Books by Julie Miller

Harlequin Intrigue

Kansas City Crime Lab

K-9 Patrol
Decoding the Truth

The Taylor Clan: Firehouse 13

Crime Scene Cover-Up
Dead Man District

The Precinct

Beauty and the Badge
Takedown
KCPD Protector
Crossfire Christmas
Military Grade Mistletoe
Kansas City Cop

Rescued by the Marine
Do-or-Die Bridesmaid
Personal Protection
Target on Her Back
K-9 Protector
A Stranger on Her Doorstep

Visit the Author Profile page at Harlequin.com.

CAST OF CHARACTERS

Chelsea O'Brien—A hacker who now works as the Kansas City Crime Lab's resident computer expert. Buck is the solid and dependable that's always been missing in her life, and she'd do anything to make the silver fox she's been crushing on notice her as more than a research asset. But will she survive going head-to-head with an enemy who's almost as good with computers as she is?

Robert "Buck" Buckner—Former KCPD cop who started his own private security firm. He can't imagine anyone less suited for him than Chelsea. She's quirky, brilliant, a decade younger and too casual with her own safety. But she's the first person to find him a lead on his missing son, and the first woman to make him consider risking his heart again. He sets all reservations aside to protect her when their investigation stirs up a threat from Chelsea's past.

Vinnie Goring—He runs the Sin City bar.

Sergeant Rufus King—Buck's former partner works at the crime lab.

Dennis Hunt—Chelsea's former boss.

Bobby Buckner—Buck's son who simply didn't come home from school one day.

Trouble—Chelsea's online stalker is bringing his threats to the real world.

Chapter One

"I found it."

Chelsea whispered the words, even though she wanted to shout them from the Sin City Bar's rooftop. Eleven months of searching every database she could legally gain access to, trolling through sites that weren't exactly in her purview as the resident computer guru of the Kansas City Police Department Crime Lab, running her own programs to keep the search going, even when she wasn't at a computer screen. Eleven months of following cyber trails to dead ends, hacking her way past them and winding up with leads to other cases she wasn't even working on. Eleven months trying to match a name, a face, a DNA profile—anything concrete. Eleven months!

She wasn't hallucinating. Even though the dim light of the bar meant she had to squint through her glasses to see her laptop, there was no mistake. Her screen was flashing that she'd found a match.

Ignoring the clink of glassware from the small kitchen behind the bar where she'd set up her laptop and Wi-Fi hot spot, she scrolled through the data again. Compared it to the information on the split screen beside it, even though she'd memorized most of the code after so many months of searching. She read the intel that jumped out at her as a solid match again.

She pushed her glasses—crystal-embedded cat-eye frames tonight—onto the bridge of her nose and confirmed it one more time.

"I found it."

Adrenaline surged up from her toes to the roots of her long brown hair and she reached into the pocket of her apron for her cell phone. She pulled up the familiar number and pushed Call.

"Hey, honey!" The scantily clad woman in the back booth scrambled off the lap of her boyfriend for the night and waved her over. She was probably freezing her giblets off in that getup on this cold, damp November night. "Bring us another round. My man's got a thirst." The woman's loud laughter ended in a squeal as the man hanging back in the shadows with her pinched something to silence her. The noise from the other patrons in the bar, namely the motorcycle club members taking up two tables near the dartboards, soon drowned out the conciliatory cooing between the couple.

Just another night at Sin City.

Tucking her phone between her shoulder and ear, Chelsea quickly poured a rum and cola, and pulled a can of lemon-lime soda from the mini-fridge. She plopped them onto a tray and carried them to the table while the phone rang. She ignored the whistles and catcalls from the bikers as she hurried past. By the time she reached the back table, the couple seemed to be scrambling to zip something into the woman's big purse and move it out of the way so that the two could sit side by side on the bench seat. If Chelsea hadn't already carded the young man, she might question whether he was underage. But he was legal. Probably more legal than his older, so-called date, who Chelsea was pretty sure would sit on any man's lap here— for the right price and the promise of a warm place to stay the night.

Chelsea nearly dropped the phone as the call connected, catching it in an awkward juggle of tray and drinks before slapping her cell back up to her ear.

"Buckner here." The man's voice was clipped to let the caller know he wasn't someone to be trifled with, laced with caution…and husky from sleep.

"Buck? It's Chelsea. I…" *Husky from sleep…* Chelsea's bubble of excitement deflated, and embarrassment swept in. "I woke you up." She glanced at her watch and cringed. "It's after midnight. I didn't think. I'm sorry."

Buck Buckner's voice, appropriately deep for the size of his broad barrel chest, cleared his throat. "That's okay. What man doesn't like a pretty woman calling him in the middle of the night?" he rumbled. "I should have checked the number before I snapped at you."

Pretty woman? With a hint of huskiness added to the deep pitch, his apology sounded unexpectedly sexy.

Sexy?

Chelsea jerked her head up to see if anyone had spotted her curious, stunned reaction. She met the irritated gaze of the young man in the corner. At least, she assumed he was irritated. His hoodie was pulled several inches past his face, casting his expression in shadows. "You gonna serve those drinks anytime tonight, four-eyes?" he prodded. Yep. Definitely irritated.

"Sure." Chelsea set the drinks on the table, and he tossed a twenty onto her tray, telling her to keep the change. Ignoring the young man's eagerness to dismiss her, she spun away to hurry back to her laptop at the bar.

"Chels?" Buck's tone sounded less drowsy. But still sexy. Rumbly and deep and definitely sexy. "Did I hear someone else? You working late?"

Wow. Since when did she associate *sexy* with Buck? And why did her fertile brain automatically take a turn into fantasyland and imagine exchanging midnight calls with Buck for an entirely different reason beyond the research she'd been doing for him this past year, as a favor to a friend with whom she worked at the crime lab?

She scooted past the drunk on the corner barstool and set her tray behind the bar. Technically, she was working, but not in the way or place he thought. "I'm alone now. I can talk."

"You called *me*?"

Buck was at least a decade older than her thirty-two years, probably more, since she knew he had a son who would be in his early twenties by now. It was hard to think of anyone she had less in common with than the brusque former cop. He commanded authority. He'd worn an army uniform, a police uniform, and now favored the uniform of a suit and tie. He ran his own business and was a well-respected man, both at KCPD and the crime lab, and in the Kansas City community. Meanwhile, she commanded computers and ran herself ragged trying to please others and stay busy enough so the lonesome mess that was her personal life didn't grab hold of her and take her down the same rabbit hole of dysfunction that had claimed her parents.

And still…

"Chels? You need to talk to me."

When he said her name like that, like it was some sort of indulgent pet name, Chelsea felt as if warm, melty chocolate was drizzling over her skin in the most sensual of ways.

She blinked rapidly, dispelling the sensation. She admired the man. Liked him as a friend. Heck, she liked him as more than a friend, but had never crossed that line because she didn't want to scare him off and risk losing him from her life. But she was pulverizing that line tonight. What was wrong with her? Were her hormones out of whack? Had her excitement over finally finding an answer for him turned her brain to mush?

She knew Buck was a divorced man and was technically available. Yes, he had taken her to breakfast many times over the past eleven months—business meetings and symbolic repayment for the time she was giving him. She'd bet she'd shared as many meals with Buck as she ate at home with her pets. He always insisted on paying and holding doors open for her. Even though she couldn't remember hearing him laugh anything more than a chuckle, his dry sense of humor could make her laugh out loud. He drove a nice truck, and had powerful shoulders, a striking dusting of silver in his short, dark hair and eyes that were a warm, golden brown.

And yeah, he had that deep, sexy voice that made her forget why she'd called him.

But while she might be totally aware of all things Buck, they weren't dating. They weren't a couple. She was an asset to him. A resource who could work her magic and give him access to a wide web of data that his limited computer skills could not. She'd volunteered for the job of helping him track down his missing son because one, she loved her technology and research and the challenge of solving an allegedly unsolvable mystery, and two, Buck had the saddest eyes she'd ever seen on a man. Eyes that held years of pain and guilt and anger. She wanted those eyes to smile. She wanted the careworn lines etched beside them to relax. If she could help him find the answers he needed, then he'd smile for her. And that would make *her* happy.

Sexy? Drizzling? Sad eyes? Where were these thoughts coming from tonight? Chelsea pinched the bridge of her nose between her thumb and finger, then nudged her glasses back into place.

She could fantasize all she wanted, but a relationship with Buck would never exist anywhere outside her imagination. Chelsea doubted Buck saw her skinny frame, myopic eyes and geeky ways as any sort of a turn-on. "It's not okay that I called so late. You work in the morning. Since I know you're a workaholic, you probably had a long day today. I doubt you ate three square meals on your own, maybe not even one. I'm sure you've had too much coffee. You need to take care of yourself and get your rest."

He snickered, but it didn't sound like he was smiling. "Well, that makes it sound like I'm halfway over the hill and need to take extra vitamins and hire a caretaker."

"I didn't mean that," she quickly apologized. "You're healthy and strong and you've got that sexy voice."

"I've got what?"

"Um…" Thank goodness the bar was dark, and the patrons were too absorbed in their own business to notice the heat flaming her cheeks. Yes, she'd said that out loud. Once again, a class in Social Skills 101 would have gone a long way to negate the effects of her damaged childhood and an adulthood spent mostly alone with her computers and pets. She exhaled an embarrassed breath. "My point is…you are not over the hill by any stretch of the imagination. You're a mature hottie. A silver fox."

He groaned.

Oh, right. She should have left out the *mature* part. Buck was 100 percent masculine, built like a Mack truck and aged like a fine wine. All that was hot. But telling a man he was hot when that wasn't the kind of relationship they shared would make things awkward between them. Not like she hadn't already made this conversation super awkward.

"Stop thinking. Start talking," Buck ordered.

Right. They'd worked together on this project long enough that he knew her weirdness like that. "It *is* rude of me to call so late."

"I'm always happy to hear from you."

"At midnight?" she scoffed. "You don't have to be nice to me."

"You don't want me to be nice to you?"

"Well, of course, I do. I wish everyone would be nice. But you know, when I insult you, whether it's intentional or not, I can still hurt your feelings or bruise your ego. You have the right to get pissed off at me. I wouldn't blame you if—"

"Chelsea. Take a breath."

She shook her head. "I'm sorry. I really shouldn't have called."

"Do you think you could go five minutes without

apologizing to me?" This time he did snap, and she knew she'd reached the end of his patience with her.

"Sorry. I do that when—"

"Chels."

"I'm s..." Do not say *sorry* again! He must already think she was a babbling idiot. But when she got excited or nervous, her thoughts went haywire, cataloging every tidbit of information and nuance of her emotional response, and her mouth followed right along with those thoughts spinning through her brain. Add in this weird crush she had on him, and she'd be hard-pressed to convince anyone she had a genius-level IQ. She'd earned her *odd bug, eccentric* and *absent-minded professor* descriptors quite honestly. She took a deep breath, as he'd advised, and got her thoughts ahead of her emotional impulses. "How about I call you in the morning after you've had your coffee."

"I'm wide-awake *now*." She heard a door opening in the background, and some water running. Splashing water on his face? Filling a glass to drink? She really had screwed this up and ruined his night. "Tell me why you called. Does this have anything to do with our little side project?"

"Yes."

"And?"

"I found him. I found your son." There was a long silence with no reply. The water ran unheeded in the background. Maybe she was wrong to get his hopes up. It wasn't every father whose son vanished from the face of the earth when he went off to college. It wasn't every father who quit his job as a Kansas City cop and started his own private investigation and security agency so he'd have more time to devote to searching for his missing son. Was Buck still there? Had he fainted? "I mean, I don't actually know *where* Bobby is. But I found his DNA. It's in a crime scene report of a John Doe murder investigation. Right here in Kansas City."

The water shut off abruptly. "Murder?"

Chelsea gestured as if Buck could see her placating him. "He's not the victim. I triple-checked before I called you."

"Thank God." She heard him exhale a sound of utter pain. "What else can you tell me?" he asked in a steely, no-nonsense voice.

"Hey, Ladybug." Vince Goring shuffled behind the bar with a tub full of dirty mugs and plopped them down beside her on the edge of the sink. The bar's owner, chief bartender and lifelong friend of Chelsea's peered at her from beneath his bushy brows and straightened with a wheezy breath. "Get another round for tables six and seven. Six drafts, one lite and a whiskey, neat."

"I'm on it, Vinnie." Chelsea patted the old man's grizzled cheek and grabbed hold of the heavy tub, indicating she'd take care of cleaning the glasses for him. Taking care of the old man who'd befriended her ages ago was a lot easier than dealing with the downward spiral of her conversation with Buck. She turned her attention back to the phone. "Hey, Buck. Sorry, I—sorry about apologizing—damn, I need to quit talking. Could we meet for breakfast tomorrow? After you've slept and I can think straight. I will fill you in on everything— what little there is—then."

She sensed Buck was on the move. Pacing? "I've been waiting four years for this. Tell me—"

"Yo, baby." Another interruption. Gordy Bismarck,

one of the rowdies who'd roared in on a fleet of motor-cycles, stomped snow and slush across the entryway rug and taken up residence at two of the high-top tables near the dartboards, shoved aside a stool in front of her and leaned over the bar. Chelsea met the rheumy eyes of the man wearing a denim jacket, sporting a patch emblazoned with the Missouri Twisters MC logo on the chest. A bandanna covered the top of his balding pate. He shoved her laptop aside. "You doin' your homework, baby girl? Checking out one of those date-a-hunk websites? Find my picture there?"

"Don't touch that!" When he started to turn the computer screen toward him, she smacked his hand, closed the screen, and hugged the laptop to her chest. In her scramble to keep the world on her computer hidden from prying eyes, she dropped her phone. Fortunately, it landed in the tub of glasses, and not the sink full of water beside it. She quickly scooped it up, wiped the dribble of warm beer off on her apron and hugged that to her chest, too. Even if she hadn't accidentally disconnected the call, Buck was probably adding *klutz* or *scatterbrain* to his opinion of her now. "Go back to your table."

Looking less than pleased that she'd struck him and rebuffed his drunken advances, the biker slunk away from the bar and jabbed a meaty finger at her. "Those mugs ain't gonna fill themselves. And you bring 'em over there yourself, baby girl. I'm tired of lookin' at the old man's ass."

"I'm not interested in whatever you're offering. Now shut your trap and go back to your game. I'll get your drinks and bring them when I'm ready."

"You need a lesson in manners."

"You think *you* can teach me some?"

Gordy grabbed the crotch of his jeans and blew a kiss at her. "I can teach you a lot, baby girl."

Chelsea frowned with disgust. "Has that line ever worked for you? Go. Away."

"Bring the damn drinks." Gordy sneered at her defiance and stormed back to his buddies at the dartboard. The ensuing mix of catcalls and cheers was loud enough to carry over the phone.

She looked at her phone to see that the call was still active, heard Buck calling her name, and with an embarrassed sigh, put it back to her ear. She cringed when he shouted her name. "I really need to get back to work."

"Who are you talking to like that? Are you hurt? Is someone threatening you?" The *sexy* was definitely gone from his tone now. Maybe she'd only imagined it earlier because that was what she'd wanted to hear.

"I'm fine." She set the laptop back on top of the bar. "I dropped my phone," she explained.

"Because someone's harassing you. Is it Hunt?"

Dennis Hunt? Her former supervisor at the Kansas City Crime Lab? Hunt was the man she was testifying against in a sexual harassment and assault case. Buck had been there the day she'd broken down and confessed everything that had happened between her and Dennis. Dennis, her former supervisor, had a proclivity for sexual harassment. But something about her must have screamed *victim* because she'd become his target for more than crude words and unwanted touches. Luckily, her new supervisor and best friend, Lexi Callahan, had risked her own safety to get Dennis arrested. The moment he'd been released on bond, Chelsea and

Lexi had both filed restraining orders against him to keep the lowlife away from them until his trial in two weeks.

"Chelsea?" Buck's voice was harsh as the former cop in him came out. "Is Hunt there? Do I need to call the police?"

Right. Because she was alone in the world, a walking magnet for trouble, and she couldn't take care of herself. Lexi had a hot cop fiancé and his K-9 partner to protect her from anything Dennis might try, but Chelsea had to be taken care of.

One of the reasons she'd been eager to help Buck with his search for his missing son was because he'd needed her. *Her.* Computer research, database knowledge, codes, programming and even hacking skills were where she could shine. She wasn't the weak link or the victim when she was working on her computer. She kicked ass and earned respect, not pity. She was the one who could help others when it came to her techno-geek skill set.

But fending off rude customers in the bar? Standing up to the man who'd assaulted her and triggered post-traumatic stress episodes? No one, not even Buck, apparently, thought she could handle herself. She wasn't sure if she was disappointed by Buck's lack of faith in her survival abilities or embarrassed to realize how much his opinion mattered to her. "Dennis isn't here. I'm not at the crime lab."

She heard movement in the background of the call. Oh, damn. He was truly wide-awake now, unnecessarily worried, and it was her fault. "Where the hell are you at this hour? Who's with you?"

"I'm at my other job. I moonlight sometimes—helping out an old friend—"

"Chelsea O'Brien!" Vinnie snapped his fingers and pointed at the scowling group of men who wanted more alcohol to fuel their evening. "Tonight, Ladybug. I don't want Gordy and his crew to be unhappy. You know they don't handle unhappy very well."

Right. This bunch had gotten into a big fight in the parking lot over a year ago. After several of them served time for it, they'd come back to their favorite haunt. "Buck, I have to go."

"*Where* are you?" He insisted on an answer.

"Sin City Bar. It's downtown. Not far from—"

"I know where it is. What the hell are you doing there? Are you okay?"

"Barkeep! Move your ass, baby girl." There was no flirting in Gordy's tone now. He didn't seem to appreciate that she'd shot him down in front of his friends. And while Chelsea could deal with anger better than unwanted lust, the demands coming at her from so many different directions flustered her.

"Are you able to talk without putting yourself in danger?" Buck demanded. "Answer yes or no. Are you okay?"

Chelsea shoved the tub out of the way and set a clean tray on the bar. "Well, I'm a little stressed out with everyone yelling at me—"

"Chelsea!" His deep breath was audible, and his volume dropped back closer to that deep-pitched huskiness. "Sweetheart, I'm sorry. Are you safe?"

Sweetheart? Why did that single word—probably a slip of the tongue that had no more meaning than Gordy Bismarck's *baby girl*—make her heart squeeze inside her chest? Oh, how she wished she'd had better role models growing up, a better understanding of normal people, so she could better understand the meaning behind why they said and did the things they did. "I have to go. Are we on for breakfast tomorrow or not?"

"I'll be there in twenty minutes."

Chapter Two

Buck had used every last curse word he knew by the time he'd raced across town as fast as the corrugated streets where snow had melted into slush and frozen into icy ruts allowed. He'd dodged a couple of slick patches, road construction and the pedestrian traffic of prostitutes, homeless people, druggies and dealers who were taking their own sweet time to get to their warm hideouts in the run-down neighborhood of No-Man's Land in downtown Kansas City.

He'd told Chelsea twenty minutes. But by the time he'd thrown on jeans, pulled on his insulated leather jacket over his shoulder holster and Glock, jumped into his truck and driven downtown, thirty minutes had passed.

He surveyed the row of motorcycles in the parking lot dusted with fresh flakes of snow as he pulled in, wondering if one of the owners had been the creep accosting Chelsea while Buck was on the phone with her. He knew a few motorcycle club members—more like gang members, in this part of town—from his time on the force. Not the company a woman like Chelsea should be keeping.

Buck assessed the three cars in the lot, identifying

one as Chelsea's red Toyota. He pulled into a spot behind it, turned his collar up against the falling snow and got out to make a quick inspection of her vehicle. No obvious car trouble like a flat tire or fluid leaking from her engine. He surveyed the rest of the lot to look for evidence of the trouble she might be in, taking note of anyone on the sidewalks or driving past. He eyed the alleyway across the street where snowdrifts clung to the shadows beside the brick walls. A bad feeling crept along the nape of his neck, prickling the short hairs there. Chelsea wasn't in her car. That meant she'd gone inside the bar. He hoped. Whatever had brought her to this part of town, he knew it was a smidge better to be safe inside a building late at night than out on the streets. Especially for a woman alone.

Buck pulled off his gloves and palmed the stubble of his jaw, steeling himself for a worst-case scenario as he strode to the bar's front door. God, he hated this neighborhood. Too many bad memories here. Homeless shelters that always seemed to be full. Underground fights. The sex trade. Drug deals. Dead bodies. Sure, there were some decent people here, broken by life, fighting for something better or simply trying to survive. But no matter how many times KCPD and the city tried to clean things up, the worst of the worst always seemed to find their way back.

Not much had changed about Sin City Bar over the years. The same rusting metal sign stained the white-painted bricks and faded awning above the heavy steel door. There were bars over the windows that looked like a row of black rectangles, since the interior was too dark to reveal much beyond the neon beer signs hanging inside. He thought of all the busts he'd made here or nearby. The lowlifes who got drunk, sold drugs or beat the crap out of each other. He knew the dive bar well from his days at KCPD. He and his partner, Rufus King, had been called here numerous times.

Even after leaving the KCPD three years ago, he'd walked these streets, searching for his son. Bobby had been a good kid, more like his mama than his tough-guy daddy. They hadn't shared many of the same interests, but Buck hadn't cared. He went to concerts and plays to support his son. He'd listened patiently and hugged his son the night Bobby had sat him and his wife, Mary, down after dinner and come out to them. In high school, when Bobby had fallen prey to bullying, Buck had stepped in to teach him ways to avoid the conflict. He'd taught him how to fight when the peaceful route failed. But his attempts to intervene only seemed to drive a wedge between them. Bobby had learned to cope by turning to drugs. He'd made some friends who Buck knew weren't on the right side of the law. Bobby had gotten sober enough to graduate high school and start a fall semester at a community college. But then one night, Buck's son simply hadn't come home.

There was no accident report. No frantic phone call for help. No crime scene with a body to identify. Bobby's abandoned car had been found in a parking lot a few blocks from here—no indication of a break-down, no signs of a struggle or other trauma. It was like he'd simply parked his car in No-Man's Land and walked away.

Bobby was gone. Vanished.

Maybe he'd run away. Maybe he'd gone back to the drugs and lost himself. Maybe he wasn't able to call for help. Or get to a police station or shelter. He knew teenage boys could fall victim to human trafficking, just like girls. He might even be dead—a John Doe like Chelsea had mentioned, with no family to claim him, to mourn him, to give him a proper funeral and celebrate his short life.

Even if Bobby was truly gone, Buck was determined to find his son and bring him home.

In the four years since the disappearance, Buck had retired from KCPD. He and Mary had divorced over the strain of losing their only child, and she had remarried a good man—a man with less grief and guilt driving him relentlessly to find the truth and keep people safe, and more time to meet her needs. He and Mary checked in with each other occasionally, but he was alone. His obsession had cost him that relationship, and he hadn't been able to sustain one since. He wasn't sure any woman would want to put up with him for the long haul.

But he had friends, like his former partner, Rufus, who now worked at the crime lab, and who had introduced him to Chelsea O'Brien. And he had Chelsea herself, the crime lab's quirky computer geek with the big green-gold eyes, a penchant for rambling, a sense of naivete and a bighearted compassion that left her vulnerable to the users and takers of the world. Like the riffraff that frequented Sin City Bar.

Losing Bobby had left a huge hole in Buck's heart.

He'd failed to protect his son.

He wasn't going to fail anybody else.

Buck pushed open the door and stepped inside the bar, pausing a moment to let his eyes adjust to the dark interior. He was instantly hit with the stale smells of alcohol and smoke that had seeped into the woodwork long before indoor smoking had been banned in the city. He pinpointed the loud, filthy-mouthed men at the high-topped tables, and the couple in the midst of make-out city in one of the back booths.

But there was no slender young woman with fun glasses, a screen of some kind at her fingertips and a perky, round butt that yeah, even at forty-five years of age, he'd have to be dead not to notice.

What was someone as sweet and clueless about the world as Chelsea doing here? And where the hell *was* she? Did he need to call his former partner for backup? Alert one of the investigators who worked for him?

He'd expect to find the nerdy, brilliant Chelsea in a campus library or coffee shop—or hell, even on a date with some equally nerdy geek her own age—not at one of Kansas City's most notorious dive bars.

She'd be easy prey for the predators who frequented the place.

And God forbid if one of those lowlifes had already hurt her…

Buck hugged his arm around the gun he carried in a shoulder holster and breathed in deeply, expanding his chest as if he was still wearing a protective uniform vest, and crossed to the bar. Since there didn't seem to be any bartender on duty, he rapped sharply on the thickly waxed pinewood top. "Anybody home?"

Chelsea herself popped up from behind the bar, nearly dropping the tub of glasses she held. "Buck?" She quickly set the tub down beside the sink behind the bar, tossed her long brown braid behind her back and pushed her sparkly glasses up on the bridge of her nose. Her eyes were wide behind her glasses, her mouth gaping open.

"What are you doing here?"

"What are you doing here?" he echoed at the same time, probably looking equally surprised to see her *working* here. She wore a black apron over her jeans and color-blocked sweater with the sleeves pushed up past her elbows. He schooled the shock out of his voice. He wanted answers. Now. "You first."

"You're wet," she stated, unaware of the impatient concern sparking through his system.

"It's snowing," he responded, swiping his hand over the top of his close-cropped hair and coming up with a palmful of melting snow that he shook off to the floor.

Chelsea freed the white towel tucked into her apron and handed it across the top of the bar for him to dry off. "I didn't think you were coming tonight."

"I said I would." Buck dried the moisture from his face and hands before setting the towel on top of the bar. He held on to his end when she picked up hers to get her full attention. Maintaining the terry cloth link forced her to tilt her gaze up to his. He wanted her to understand that she didn't belong in a place like this. "You can't tell me you're at Sin City and expect me *not* to show up."

"I'm fine here, Buck. Really. I mean, most of the time I am."

"*Most* of the time? This is a regular haunt of yours?" A protective fury heated his blood. What kind of reassurance was that supposed to be? "I've carted people off in handcuffs and sent them away in ambulances from this place." He tugged on the towel, pulling her as close as the bar between them allowed. "We need to leave."

The gray-haired drunk sitting at the far end of the bar pulled his nose up out of his empty highball glass where it looked like he'd been dozing, and turned his barstool toward Buck. "This your daddy come to take you home, Chel-shee?"

"Go back to sleep, Martin." Chelsea gently reprimanded the man with the slurred speech before yanking the towel from Buck's unresisting grip and tucking it back into the waistband of her apron. "I can't leave yet. Not until closing."

Martin Buttinsky wagged a knowing finger at Buck and winked at Chelsea—although the wink turned into a double blink. "He's your *sugar* daddy."

Buck needed this conversation to be private again. "Take a hike, pal."

"She's all yours." This time, the blinky wink was aimed toward Buck. "I've been trying to pick her up for ten years." It took a couple of tries, but he touched his finger to his nose in that sign of shared knowledge. "She's a challenge. Never goes home with anyone."

Buck swung his gaze back to Chelsea. "You've been working here for ten years? Doesn't the state pay you enough for your work at the crime lab?"

"I don't get paid to work here, unless someone forgets himself and leaves me a tip." She thought a lone woman coming to No-Man's Land late at night was a sensible volunteer calling? The way Chelsea's mind worked was completely baffling. But he was beginning to see that she seemed to think her time here was exactly that—some kind of *calling* to help people. She slipped to the end of the bar where the old man sat. "Could I get you a cup of coffee, Martin?"

He sat up straight, slurring his indignant reply. "Why don't you just tell me to leave if that's how you're going to treat me."

Taking no offense, Chelsea hurried around the corner of the bar to help steady the man as he got up off his barstool and lurched toward the door. "Walking or driving?" she asked.

"No gas in the car. Walking."

"Good. Because I was going to take your keys." She dipped into her tip apron and pressed some money into his hand. "Here. Catch the bus up at the corner. Put your gloves on and wrap that scarf around your neck. Don't spend that on more booze. Go home."

Martin's gaze seemed to clear for a split second before he squeezed her fingers and thanked her for the handout. "You're good people, Shelsea," he slurred.

"Take care of yourself." She walked him to the door, cringing against the gust of cold wind that blew in when she opened the door and sent him on his way.

Although the urge to intervene jolted through Buck's legs, he realized the drunk wasn't the threat here. Even if there was any truth to his claim of hitting on Chelsea, she'd handled him just fine. Buck was more worried about the rest of the bar's clientele, who wouldn't be satisfied with a kind word or a small handout. He used the opportunity to scan the bikers to see if he recognized any of them from past arrest records. There were a few familiar faces. And none of the ones he recognized had been arrested for anything as benign as jaywalking. The bald one with the bandanna tied over his head met Buck's astute gaze and doffed him a salute before laughing at something one of his compatriots had said and turning back to his darts game. Gordy something. He remembered him from a domestic violence call. He'd file away the name for now and call Rufus for some intel about the losers who frequented this place.

"I guess you couldn't wait until tomorrow to find out what I learned." He almost startled at Chelsea's voice near his shoulder as she skirted past him in a waft of lemon soap and cold, fresh air to go back to work behind the bar.

"No way was I going back to sleep. First, you drop the bombshell about my son. And then you tell me you're in this place? I was worried." He braced his elbows on the top of the bar and leaned closer. "Sin City's got a reputation, and it's not a good one."

Those big hazel eyes collided with his. "You thought I was in trouble?"

Could she not see how out of place she was here? How much danger she could be in? And what the hell was that flip-flop of something softening inside him at that beautiful gaze meeting his? "Yeah."

"No one ever comes to my rescue." She hugged the mug she'd been washing to her chest. "That's really sweet."

"Sweet. Yeah, that's what I was going for."

She missed his stab at sarcasm. "It is?"

"No." He pushed away from the bar. Although his hackles were still up about everything and everyone surrounding Chelsea in this place, he toned down the Terminator-to-the-rescue vibe that had spurred him across the city to get to her. He was getting too old to play hero, and she didn't seem to want him to, anyway.

But still, she'd called him with the first news about Bobby he'd had in years. He didn't intend to wait for breakfast or even another hour to find out what she'd learned. "Look, I'll take you up on that cup of coffee if it's fresh, the mug is clean, and that riffraff stays on their side of the bar." He nodded toward the bikers who were getting drunker and louder by the minute, before tilting his head toward her. "Could we talk?"

After a quick glance around the bar to at least acknowledge the potential threat here, she nodded. She poured two mugs of coffee and set them on the counter as he pulled out a barstool. "Straight up and hot enough to burn your gullet."

"Just the way I like it." They'd shared enough breakfasts together that she knew the way he took his coffee.

She doctored hers with a shot of cream before coming around to where he'd pulled out the barstool beside him. Buck tensed as the door behind the bar swung open and a stoop-shouldered man carrying two six-packs of longneck beers stepped out.

The older man's eyes narrowed as he studied Buck's bulky frame standing across from him. "I know you. You're a cop." Looking none too pleased by Buck's arrival, the bar's owner loaded the beers into the refrigerator beside the cash register on the back wall. "Who's done what now?"

"Former cop," Buck corrected. "Twenty years was all I could handle." He pulled out his ID to show the other man. "I remember you, Mr. Goring. I'm a private investigator now. Run my own security firm. I'm here to see Chelsea."

"Well, I know she ain't done nothin' wrong." Goring pointed a gnarled finger at Chelsea. "You okay, Ladybug? This guy bothering you?"

"I'm fine, Vinnie. Buck is my friend." She glanced up at Buck, and he could see another one of her apologies forming on her lips. "I mean. We're working together on a project—"

"I'm a friend." It seemed right to stand up for her in this place, to claim a connection to her. To let the old man and the drunk who might have taken advantage of her big heart and the leches eyeing her from the dart game across the way know that she wasn't alone in this place, that she had someone watching her back. As far as Buck was concerned, they *were* more than coworkers on a special project. He enjoyed the time he spent with Chelsea. He knew she'd been through hell growing up, and more recently in an incident at the crime lab last year. But it hadn't warped her. Her resilience gave him hope that he'd be able to get through however the outcome of his search for Bobby ended up. She was funny and brilliant, quirky but kind, and she surprised him in some way almost every time they met. "I'm a *good* friend."

Vinnie Goring nodded skeptically. "Uh-huh."

Chelsea pulled her gaze from Buck to address her apparent boss. "Things are winding down until we need to finish cleanup. I'm taking a break to talk to Buck, okay?"

"That what you want?" Vinnie asked.

She rested a hand on Buck's forearm and nodded. "He's a good guy."

"Holler if you need anything." Her words seemed to appease the old man, and he disappeared back through the swinging door.

At least, she had someone looking out for her here. Although Buck wasn't sure how much protection a gray-haired man stooped with arthritis could offer. He settled onto the barstool and looked down at Chelsea. "How do you know Vince Goring? He a relative?"

"No." She rolled her mug between her hands, maybe warming her fingers, maybe buying a little time to answer his questions. "Vinnie needed help. He had knee replacement surgery in September. It's still hard for him to get around. He can't run this place by himself and, as you can probably imagine, it's hard to hire anyone reliable who'll stay for very long."

"I can imagine. But why *you*?"

"I've known Vinnie since I was ten years old. He's like a favorite uncle or grandfather to me." She lifted the coffee to her lips, let the steam fog up her glasses, then took them off to clean them with the towel at her waist before settling them back onto her nose. She was stalling for time. Whatever she was going to explain to him wasn't easy for her. "My parents were alcoholics. As they lost job after job and money got tight, this became their watering hole. The drinks were even cheaper back then. Sometimes, when Mom and Dad didn't come home, I'd have to come and get them."

Buck's hand curled into a fist on top of the bar. "You came into this dump as a child? Into this neighborhood?"

She finally looked up from the coffee she wasn't drinking. "Not all of us come from the suburbs or downtown lofts, Buck. Mom and Dad lost the house in Independence, and we moved into an apartment a few blocks from here. We even spent time at the homeless shelter over on Yankee Hill Road. Until Mom and

Dad got kicked out for being drunk. Then I went into foster care."

Buck swore under his breath. He'd give anything to have his son back in his life. To know he was alive. To take care of him. He couldn't imagine a childhood like Chelsea was describing. "I'm so sorry."

"There are good parts to this story, too." She traced her fingertip around the rim of her mug, and Buck couldn't help but notice how delicate and graceful her hand seemed next to his bear paw. "Like Vinnie. He would help me get Mom and Dad on the bus. Or, when I turned sixteen and got my license, I'd drive them home. Of course, I was in foster care by then. Not supposed to have contact with them. But they needed me. I was already pretty good with tech. I had an unregistered phone to talk to them on, even before I knew what a burner phone was. I was here once or twice a week. Less often as I got older. Until they died in a car wreck."

"Sounds rough."

She nodded. "Foster care was rough."

Buck reached out and laid his hand over hers where it fisted in her lap. He knew that she'd been sexually abused by one of her foster parents—he'd learned about it after a sexual assault incident with her former supervisor at the crime lab last year that had triggered a PTSD episode in Chelsea.

He wasn't sure why—maybe simply because he was the one who had been there to pick her up for breakfast for an update on her research—but she'd confessed both the past trauma and how that bastard at work had cornered her in his office and attempted to rape her. The assault had set off a violent response, which the man had initially used to blackmail her into silence. Although Buck's first instinct after hearing all the details was to plow his fist through Dennis Hunt's face, he'd held her until the tears had subsided. Then he'd taken Chelsea to a friend of hers at the lab, and she'd helped Chelsea make the necessary reports to get the man arrested. Now Hunt was awaiting trial on multiple assault and harassment charges.

Buck wondered if facing Hunt again in a courtroom would trigger another episode. He wondered if she had anyone besides Vinnie the bartender in her life to back her up when she had to face something as difficult as testifying. Was she getting the counseling she needed? He tightened his grip around her hand. What was it about this woman that made him go into defender mode? He'd been worried about the troublemakers of the Sin City Bar hurting her—but she had demons of her own to battle that were far worse. Maybe she'd been focused on simply surviving for so long, that she wasn't even aware of the threats surrounding her that he saw so clearly. Could he be the support system she needed? If she found Bobby for him, he'd do anything she asked, be whatever she needed him to be.

Hell. Even if he never saw his son again, he wanted to take care of her.

"Why do I find it so easy to tell you these things?"

When she looked at him like that, Buck admitted that this drive to protect Chelsea wasn't only about his need for her help in finding his son, or his old-school notions about how a man should treat a woman. He liked her—the cosmic intelligence in those eyes, the curvy butt, the sly humor, the gentle smile. She brought laughter and hope into his dark, cynical world. Chelsea wasn't a conventional beauty, but something about her spoke to him in a way that no woman had since he had fallen in love with his ex-wife so many years ago.

Whoa. *Dial it back a notch, stud.* What did he think he had in common with Chelsea that could warrant the word *love* even entering his thoughts? He had some gray in his hair, like Vinnie—the man she'd described as a favorite uncle or grandfather—even though he was certain the man was at least twenty years his senior. After her experiences with abuse and harassment, she probably thought of him as another father figure, a safe man to have in her life.

If he was ever going to fall in love again, he didn't want to be with a woman because she thought he was *safe*. He wanted passion. He wanted the crazy monkey sex where they couldn't keep their hands off each other. He wanted that soul-deep connection that he'd known for a few years with his ex-wife. He wanted that infinite trust, the shared secrets and private jokes. He wanted to be the one man she couldn't live without.

Yeah, that kind of reality certainly put the damper on whatever attraction his tired brain and body were conjuring about Chelsea tonight.

He released a wry chuckle. "You talk to me because I'm the guy who's here when you need to talk."

"It's more than timing. I feel safe opening up to you."

Yep. There was the dreaded word. *Safe.* He had absolutely no business being interested in anything romantic or sexual with this woman. Friends and coworkers. That was all they were. That was all he needed them to be. He should remember that fact and let go of her hand.

But Chelsea laced her fingers with his before summoning a sentimental smile and continuing. "Vinnie looked out for me when I was here. He'd make a space where I could do my homework or read while Mom and Dad sobered up enough to leave. Later, he'd let me hang out when I had to get out of that house." Her fingers pulsed within his grip, and Buck knew what she meant by *that house*. "Vinnie is the one who convinced me that I had to report Mr. Leighton to my social worker. He was with me when I called her. This is where she picked me up, and I never went back to that house again. I owe him."

"I'm revising my opinion of Vinnie. However, this still is no place for you to be working." He pointed out the various clientele who seemed intent on closing the place down. "Gang fights. Drug deals. The couple having sex in the last booth."

Chelsea's soft laugh teased his eardrums despite the raucous swell in volume over a bull's-eye shot at the dartboards. "I don't think it's gone that far," she pointed out. "Mostly, he sits there like he's hiding from the world and plays games on his phone or computer pad. She laughs. He shushes her. They kiss. Then it all starts over again." She leaned into Buck's shoulder and whispered. "She's a hooker."

Buck arched an eyebrow, thinking the thigh-high boots and barely-there miniskirt that were wildly inappropriate for a Missouri winter—along with the hard look of the streets about her eyes—made that a pretty good guess. Although Buck had recognized several of the bikers, he couldn't place the young man in the back booth. But then, the couple had probably chosen the shadows and partitions at the back of the bar for privacy. Even if he got a good look, he'd been out of law enforcement going on three years now. "Is he a regular, too?"

"He was in here a couple of times before, with a different girl. Same make-out session. His name is TJ. He looks young enough that I carded him. Both times, when I took his order, he slapped two one-hundred-dollar bills on the table to buy a round of drinks for everyone here on the condition that they'd be left alone." Her shoulders shook with a dramatic shiver. "Gordy and his buddies were happy to oblige for the round of beers. Frankly, I was happy to serve the drinks and walk away. I wasn't too sure what I'd be seeing back there."

"Sounds wise." From what Buck could see the young man's clothes were a lot nicer than the woman crawling over him. Probably slumming. Or cheating on a wife or girlfriend who wouldn't do the dirty stuff he wanted. Buck swallowed the bile rising in his gullet. "The fact that you know names and that sort of information about your patrons worries me."

She laughed louder at that, and the sound made him smile. "You'd be surprised by what I know, Buck."

Chapter Three

Buck's urge to smile vanished. What kind of first-hand knowledge about the criminals and lowlifes hanging out at Sin City was Chelsea talking about? Was she saying she *had* run into danger here? "Find another way to help Vinnie. This isn't safe."

"If you're going to lecture me, you might as well leave, and I won't tell you what I found out." Chelsea was the one to finally pull away, breaking even that casual contact of holding hands. He couldn't look away as she pushed aside her coffee and dangled over the top of the bar like a gymnast to retrieve something on the other side. His pulse fired like a teenager's at the sight of her lush, curvy bottom bobbing in the air.

It fired with something hotter when he saw that Gordy Bald Biker Guy had noticed her derriere squirming in the air, too. "Chels."

Was any break on the investigation worth the threats surrounding her here?

Buck pushed to his feet and grabbed Chelsea at either side of her waist, easily lifting her and pulling her back down to the barstool. His mood darkened as he glared across the room at the biker, daring him to keep eyeballing Chelsea like she was a tasty treat he wanted to sample. When Gordy's eyes met his, the biker laughed, looking amused by Buck's protective stance. But he wised up and raised his hands in surrender, turning his focus back to his buddies.

Chelsea seemed completely oblivious to the silent interchange of testosterone as she opened the laptop she'd retrieved to pull up information on her screen.

"This is why you're here. I've been running cases with unmatched DNA through multiple databases." She pointed to a lab report from the Kansas City Police Department, then pulled up another screen beside it, which Buck recognized as Bobby's DNA profile the Kansas City Crime Lab had put together from samples taken from some of Bobby's toiletries after his disappearance. "I won't explain the logistics of how I finally tracked this down, but your son's DNA matches a DNA sample in that report."

Once he was certain that Gordy's interest had shifted away from Chelsea, Buck leaned in to read the information over her shoulder. "This crime report is from last year."

"I've gone back through the past four years of records, since just before you filed the missing person report on Bobby." He'd been hoping for something more recent. Something more concrete. Then again, he'd been hoping for *any* news about his son. "Local. State. National. Genealogy websites. Declassified documents. So far, I've drawn the line at hacking into anything that could get me into trouble at work. There's been some recent activity on Bobby's social media page. I'm pretty sure the posts aren't his, though. His isn't the first account to get hacked. I even trolled some chat rooms and dating apps." She nodded toward the screen. "I've gotten nothing concrete on Bobby until this popped up tonight."

"The people online in those places can't track your search back to you, can they?"

"I'm pretty good at what I do," she stated matter-of-factly. "Use an alias, bounce the signal off different IP addresses. Throw in misdirection and roadblocks. I'm a ghost out there."

He didn't understand half of what she'd said, but he knew she'd taken a risk on his behalf. Maybe as big a risk as working nights at this dump. "I know you're better than *pretty good.* But let's keep my worry meter down and keep things legal and safe for now, shall we?" He squeezed her shoulder to thank her for all her time-consuming work. "Show me what you've got."

Buck read the information on her screen. It was a John Doe murder outside the Lukinburg Embassy in the international trade area of Kansas City. An unidentified man found dead in his car, garroted from behind. A quick glimpse of the images as Chelsea scrolled through the information told him this guy was somebody. Youngish, but dressed in a tailored suit and tie. "Nobody has stepped forward to identify him? It's not like he's a vagrant off the street. His nails are clean. His skin isn't leathery from too much time out in the elements. That car is parked in front of the embassy. Does he work there? Was he visiting someone?" He read the small print in one of the windows she'd pulled up. "You accessed Interpol files?"

Chelsea pushed up her glasses and clicked through the information on the screen as if the depth of her talent was no big thing. "The embassy says he's not an employee, and if he was a Lukinburg national, he hadn't checked in with the embassy yet. I'm running a passport search to see if he matches anyone entering the country. But since I'm relying on facial recognition, it could take a while. If he's in the country illegally, a match might never pop."

"Maybe he was on his way to the embassy for help but didn't get there in time." He muttered a curse, remembering some cases from his time at KCPD. "Lukinburg had a pretty significant organized crime system—as deep and violent as the Russian mob."

Chelsea averted her gaze from the graphic image on the screen. "That would explain that type of murder."

"You're not pinging on some mob radar, are you?" But just as quickly as worry kicked his pulse into over-time, he inhaled a calming breath and shook his head. "The corrupt government officials have been ousted, and legit businessmen and politicians are being sup-ported now. They've even got a new king who doesn't shy away from improving his country's reputa-tion." And he knew one thing with certainty. "Bobby wouldn't be a part of anything like that."

Thankfully, she didn't try to argue that his son had become a professional killer. "The victim doesn't match any missing person reports in the area. The au-topsy revealed he had narcotics in his system, but he wasn't a chronic user. Not a known dealer, either. The lab is trying to identify him through dental records. But they haven't found any matches in KC or Missouri."

"He's from somewhere else." That would be the hy-pothesis Buck would pursue if he was on the case. Expand the search to other databases. Explore the in-ternational connections.

Chelsea had the same idea. "I can expand my search

of dental records. But I'd need probable cause and a request from the investigators to do it legally. If he is a Lukinburger, then it falls under their jurisdiction, and the State Department would want to know why I was getting involved. Lukinburg is a big trade partner with the US. He could be from any state, or almost any country, if he was there to do business with someone at the embassy."

"Maybe the killer is trying to make his murder look like something bigger than it is." Buck settled back onto the stool beside her, scanning the report more carefully. "It'd be a smart way to throw off the authorities looking into his death. Turn what could be a personal dispute or a local hit into an international incident and ignore a simpler, domestic explanation." He scrubbed his hand over his jaw, frustrated by the lack of actual details in the report. "Tell me how Bobby's DNA showed up in this mess?"

Chelsea switched screens and pointed to an image of the victim's clothes spread out on an examination table in the lab. Circles had been drawn around two small stains on the lapel and cuff of the suit jacket. "They found his DNA on the victim's suit, not in the wound track or anywhere else in the car. Could he have been a friend of Bobby's? Maybe he borrowed your son's clothes."

Buck shook his head. "His build is too different for Bobby's clothes to fit him. Once he got off the drugs, Bobby filled out. By graduation, he was a big kid, stocky like his dad." Buck thumped his chest to indicate the difference between his son and this man's slender build. "I don't recognize him. Of course, those last few months, I didn't realize Bobby was in trouble again. I knew he was seeing someone he met on campus. But I never met the young man."

Chelsea pointed to the date on the screen. "This murder happened last October. So, you know Bobby was alive and in the KC area at least through that time. Chances are, he still is."

Buck nodded. He absolutely wanted to believe that his son was still alive. If this man could be identified, he'd have a whole new avenue to investigate—acquaintances of the victim, coworkers, any mutual enemies he might have shared with Bobby. But until that ID was made, this information didn't put him any closer to finding his son and holding him in his arms again.

"I know finding his DNA at a crime scene isn't what you were hoping for, but at least it's proof of life. Up until thirteen months ago, at any rate."

"Do the police suspect him of killing this person?"

"I don't know. This is the lab report, not the investigator's file. Finding a match for the DNA might be KCPD's first lead. At this point, they've probably turned it over to the cold case team. That's Lieutenant Rafferty-Taylor's unit." Buck knew the woman who ran the cold case squad. Ginny Rafferty-Taylor was a smart, thorough investigator. He turned his focus to Chelsea when she lightly cleared her throat. "I will need to report my findings to the investigative team, tell them I matched the DNA sample. Along with the other matches I found."

"You found Bobby's DNA at other crime scenes?" Buck felt a little sick that he had to ask the question.

"No." Chelsea squeezed his forearm, hastening to reassure him. "Not Bobby's. But my online digging has turned up matches to three other investigations where the DNA on file was previously unidentified. It's a search algorithm I came up with."

"You've dug up four matches?"

She nodded but didn't seem overly pleased by her success. "Either I've gotten extraordinarily lucky or something weird is going on. The statistics are a little wonky to suddenly have this kind of success."

He doubted luck had anything to do with it. "You're too smart for your own good, O'Brien. Hopefully, these new DNA matches will give the detectives the leads they need to close those cases."

"I hope it's not a glitch in the system that will send them off on a wild-goose chase, following false leads."

"KCPD will be looking for Bobby as a person of interest now, not a missing person. Even at the worst of his addiction, Bobby was a gentle soul. If this was a boyfriend he'd argued with, or a hookup gone wrong, he still wouldn't commit murder." Buck couldn't wrap his head around what all this meant yet. "Unless it was self-defense."

But a garrote from behind was certainly no defensive injury.

"Don't go there." Chelsea leaned toward him and squeezed his thigh. Buck felt an unexpected jolt right up to his groin and silently cursed his base reaction. The woman was trying to console him, and his body was reacting as if she was coming on to him—and he liked it. "There are a lot of reasons why Bobby's DNA might be at the crime scene. Maybe the victim knew Bobby, and the stains came from an earlier encounter. Maybe Bobby used to live in the victim's apartment. Or they had a class together. Maybe Bobby spilled his drink on him at a bar or...anything. Once we ID the victim, I can run all kinds of searches to find the connection between them. I should have the passport results sometime tomorrow."

Buck rested his big hand over hers. Beyond the frissons of an ill-timed sexual attraction that wouldn't go away, there was something soothing in Chelsea's touch, something infinitely hopeful in her defense of a young man she'd never met. This woman was a ray of sunlight in Buck's dark, broody world, and he craved her company the way a prisoner craved daylight.

But since she was probably closer to his son's age than she was to his, Buck refused to act on the feelings she stirred inside him. He raised her fingers to his lips, kissed her knuckles, then released her and stood.

"Can you run me a copy of the police report on that John Doe? I'll follow up with some of my own contacts."

She nodded. "Stop by the lab tomorrow, and I'll have it for you. Or I can send a copy to your phone right now." He rolled his eyes and she smiled. "Someday, you're going to have to let me show you how that thing works. Bring you into the twenty-first century and teach you all the technology at your fingertips."

"Someday, you're going to have to stop calling me from dive bars in the middle of the night and make me think you're in trouble."

She laughed outright at that. "I'll check my watch before I call you next time."

"Anytime you need me, you call." He pulled a bill from his wallet and set it on the counter for the coffee.

"Coffee's always on the house."

When she scooted the ten-dollar bill aside, he scooted it back. Even if Chelsea wouldn't take it, he wanted to repay the owner in some small way for looking out for her. "Will Mr. Goring walk you to your car after closing?"

"Vinnie lives upstairs."

Not what he asked. "When does the bar close?"

"One thirty. Vinnie should be doing last call any time now."

A half hour until closing. Time enough to read through the details of that crime scene report. "Thank you. For everything. I'll let you get back to work."

"I'll see you tomorrow at the lab."

"I'm not going anywhere." When she started to question that promise, he pressed a finger against her lips and shushed her. Even as his sensitive fingertip was memorizing the soft give of her bottom lip, he pulled away and tapped his chest. "Old-school alpha male. You walk a lady to her car late at night—make sure she gets there safely."

He watched the couple from the back booth stumble out of their seats and stagger toward them. The young man's logoed hoodie was either a knock-off, stolen, or a pricey investment that was way out of place in this part of town. That hoodie, and his dedication to leaving a hickey on the blonde woman's neck, masked most of his face as he spoke to Chelsea. "Into computers, huh?" He pulled the strap of his date's messenger bag up onto her shoulder and hugged her to his side. "Seems out of place in a dump like this."

"But you were on your pad—"

"Time for you to get home, son." Buck cut off her argument.

"Okay, Pop." The young man snorted his disrespect

before waving to Chelsea. "I left a little tip on the table for you, honey. I'm saving my big tip for Desiree here."

The woman who seemed older than the guy up close cackled. "You're so funny, TJ."

She grabbed the young man's butt, and he growled. "It ain't no joke, baby. Big."

The woman screeched another laugh at the crude words and touches TJ was dishing out. Chelsea averted her head, her cheeks coloring with an unexpected blush.

Was she embarrassed? Offended? Wishing she didn't haven't to be a witness to the overtly public make-out session? Buck stepped between Chelsea and the handsy couple. "You two need to find a private room somewhere else. There's a lady present."

"Mine or yours?"

Buck didn't find the twentysomething hotshot nearly as funny as he seemed to find himself. Comparing Chelsea to a hooker? Hell, even Desiree needed to find a man who respected her more than this. Bracing his hands at his waist to push out his shoulders and block Chelsea from view, Buck stared down the younger man. He felt Chelsea's hand splay at the small of his back, and her touch jolted through him. Was she urging him to be calm, worried he was going to start a fight? Or was she clinging to him because TJ's insults were getting under her skin?

Buck's cop-protector-security-specialist-badder-than-you-could-ever-hope-to-be stance got the kid moving toward the door. "I'm going, Pop. I'm goin'. C'mon, D."

"Big tip." Desiree giggled. "I get it."

The couple stumbled out the door because they couldn't keep their hands to themselves.

"She's a real candidate for Mensa," Chelsea quipped, pulling her hand away.

Although he regretted the loss of her touch, Buck's lips curved with the urge to laugh at her snarky comment. "You carded him, right?"

"Of course." Chelsea circled around the bar to dip a cloth into the sudsy sink water and squeeze it until it was damp. "He's legal. His license said he was twenty-four."

Not much older than Bobby. Judging by the jacket and Doc Martens on his feet, the young man either made good money, or came from it. What was he doing here in No-Man's Land, instead of spending the night at a college hangout or preppy sports bar with someone his own age? And why would he hire himself a date? Was this some kind of fraternity initiation? Then again, maybe the kid's money wasn't legit. Maybe he'd come to this part of the city to sell drugs to an embarrassingly robust market.

He hated that Chelsea was working here. "I don't think any of the bozos here are going to walk you to your car. Unless you've got somebody else waiting for you?"

"Like a boyfriend?" Her cheeks blushed an adorable shade of pink before she flashed him a smile. "I don't."

Nope. That news shouldn't have made him grin like an idiot inside. Buck was not boyfriend material. Not for this woman.

"Then, refill my coffee, barkeep." He pulled her laptop over in front of the stool where he'd been sitting. "I'll stay out of the way and do some reading while you finish up."

Chelsea wagged her finger at him. "How about I

brew you a fresh pot of decaf. I have a feeling you've drunk more than the legal limit of fully-leaded coffee today. Your body needs a break."

"Cutting me off?" She beamed at his teasing, and Buck felt like he was ten feet tall for putting that smile on her lips.

"I'm taking care of the people who are important to me."

She disappeared into the back room. He was important to her? His stomach lining, his ability to sleep, and his ego all appreciated her concern. Buck couldn't help but slide his glance over to Gordy What's-his-face, who still seemed to think that Chelsea's business was his business, and let the tattooed fool know that *Buck* was the man who could make Chelsea smile. *Buck* was the one who was getting some special treatment from her. And *Buck* would be the one walking her to her car when the night was done.

Thirty minutes later, the bikers had ridden away in a noisy roar of machinery. Vinnie and Chelsea cleaned the tables and removed all the dirty glasses and mugs from the bar. Buck set chairs and stools up on tables and the bar so that Vinnie could sweep the place. The snow had let up to an occasional snowflake drifting through the air by the time the older man kissed Chelsea's cheek and locked the door behind them.

Buck's truck and Chelsea's car were the only vehicles left in the dimly lit parking lot. But there was still some traffic rolling by, still some pedestrians trailing out of other closing nightspots and fleabag hotel rooms in the area. Buck was glad he didn't have to think about Chelsea walking across the empty expanse of asphalt this time of night by herself.

With his fingers shoved into the pockets of his jacket to curtail the urge to settle a hand at the small of her back, beneath the computer backpack she'd heaved onto the shoulder of a bulky tweed coat that had to have come from the men's section of a thrift shop, he simply walked beside her. Although he swept the street, sidewalk and parking lot for any signs of movement or interest in them, he also noticed how the top of Chelsea's head matched up to the square jut of his chin, and he felt like a big ol' grizzly bear walking beside a delicate forest doe.

Nothing in common with this woman, he reiterated to himself. Too young. Too fragile. Too naive and trusting.

"How old are you, Chels?" The question came out before he had a chance to filter his thoughts through common sense and consideration.

She snorted what he supposed was a laugh. "How old do you think I am?"

Now that he'd started the conversation, he erred on the side of not offending her. "About the same age as that rude kid with the hot date. Twenty-five?"

Chelsea stopped in her tracks. Buck moved two steps beyond before he realized it, and he turned to face her amused expression. "Thank you, but, um, I'm thirty-two."

Thirty-two. Still a thirteen-year age gap between them. But he didn't feel quite so guilty about his fascination with her. They were both adults with a little life experience to them—hell, they probably had more experience between them than most folks endured in a couple of lifetimes. Still nothing in common, though, beyond the search for his son.

"Why do you ask?" she prodded, catching up to him with her keys ready to unlock her car.

"You seem so hopeful about people, so trusting. Especially with all you've been through, you're—"

"A Pollyanna?" She clicked the remote.

"I was going to say *amazing*."

"You were?" Her cheeks turned pink as she spotted a soggy, folded piece of heavy paper beneath her windshield wiper and pulled it free. "I think it's the whole nearsighted, absentminded geek vibe I give off. I choose to be hopeful because I know how dark the world can be, and I can't live in that kind of place. Too many freckles and a skinny body make me seem young, too."

Skinny? With that perfect butt? It probably wasn't wise to argue curves with her, so he chose another point. "Most people would be pretty jaded if they went through everything you have."

She dusted off the snow as she unfolded the paper to read it. "I don't trust easily, Buck. I can count on one hand the number of people I do trust." She wiggled her fingers in the air. "You're one of these."

"I'm honored." He reached around her to open the door but stopped when her smile vanished and her cheeks went pale. "Chels?"

She turned the paper over and held it up toward the dim light from the nearest streetlamp for him to read.

Buck's blood steamed in his veins. It was a picture of her. Same outfit she was wearing right now. Taken outside this very bar, probably as she'd headed in to work earlier this evening. Someone had scribbled a message over the black-and-white printout. The rain had smeared the ink, but the threat was succinct and to the point.

Stop what you're doing. Or someone will get hurt.

"I don't know what that means. Stop what? Who's he going to hurt?"

Buck glimpsed a tiny flare of light from the alleyway across the street and reacted instinctively. By the time he heard the pops of a gun being fired, he'd dragged Chelsea up against his chest and twisted her away from the shots. He dove for the pavement a split second before her windshield exploded.

Chapter Four

The pops kept coming. Chelsea lost count after the fifth shot.

"What the hell is happening?" she shouted against Buck's neck.

"Someone's shooting at us," he growled.

"Duh." She flinched beneath him as another window exploded and glass rained down over them. "Why?"

"Survive first, answers later."

Her left elbow burned, and she could barely catch her breath with Buck's full weight pressing her down onto the asphalt. She felt the pinch of every tiny piece of gravel poking into her bottom and thighs, and her wool coat and jeans were soaking up the slush that had melted in the parking lot. But other than a slight case of dizziness at having been taken down so quickly, she hadn't struck her head or been hit by a bullet or the broken glass.

Because Buck's big hands cradled her head. Her face was tucked against the juncture of his neck and shoulder, her panicked breaths filling her nose with the faint piney scent of soap from his warm skin. His arms had whipped around her, absorbing the brunt of the fall, even as he shielded her from flying bullets and shattering glass above them.

She should be feeling something else at this shoulder-to-toe contact. Something she inevitably felt every time a man had put his hands on her since she'd been a preteen girl. That flare of panic that engulfed her almost every time a man pressed himself against her. Years of counseling had helped. Knowing the man who'd hurt her was in prison helped. But she struggled with the flashbacks sometimes when she was caught unawares.

Buck's thigh was wedged squarely between hers in a position that could only be more intimate if they were naked. A few layers of clothing were all that separated her squished breasts from the hard wall of his chest, and nothing separated his heat from her.

Yes, the hail of bullets tearing up her car and the shattering glass was frightening. But her thoughts detached, as they sometimes did when she got overly stressed. It was a coping mechanism she'd learned years ago. Why wasn't she panicking at being pinned down like this? Was it because she logically knew this was the best way to shield her body out in the open like this? Or did it have something to do with Buck himself? The man was practically surrounding her body. She felt a rush of awareness, yes, a recognition of a man's strength and heat aligning to her meager curves. But there was no fear of the man. She felt relief. Security. It was something she'd never believed she would truly be able to feel.

Like she belonged in this man's arms.

Her wandering thoughts came back into sharp focus when the shooting finally stopped. Threat. Bullets. Glass. Buck.

She lay in the solid, warm cocoon of Buck's body until the last tinkling of glass shards found their resting place on the pavement around them. They shared deep, measured breaths as their bodies melded together. There was blessed silence for a split second before she heard the roar of a motorcycle starting up and racing away, and Buck's muttered curse.

"Buck?" she whispered, fearful of what that curse might mean. Just as she'd recognized her body's awareness of being surrounded by a whole lot of potent male, a slew of more important observations put her on wary alert. Something warm and liquid dripped onto her cheek. Blood? Not hers. "Buck?" She fisted her hands in his jacket and pushed some space between them. He was hurt. How badly? Fear, more powerful than her reaction to the first gunshot or her trepidation over the creepy note swelled within her. Even with her arms wedged between them, she tried to shake a response out of him. She ran her fingertips along his stubbled neck and jaw, whatever she could reach. "You're bleeding. Did you get shot?"

With one arm cinched around her to keep her body close to his, Buck pushed himself up on one hand. Like snow being swept off the hood of her car, a million bits of glass rained down around them as Buck hauled her up to a sitting position. Her chest expanded with a welcome deep breath, but her fists still clung to the front of Buck's jacket, holding tight as he shrugged off more of the glass. He went out of focus as he pulled back and sank onto one knee beside her.

"Buck?" For a split second she panicked at her world blurring, until she realized she'd lost her glasses in their tumble. But she didn't need twenty-twenty vision to get this job done. Chelsea curled her legs beneath her and pushed up onto her knees, leaning toward him and squinting to get a better look at the slash of crimson carved across his cheek. "Oh my God."

He pulled her fingers away and gently turned her arm, inspecting the shredded wool and blood oozing through the elbow of her sweater. "Where are you hit?"

"I'm not. You are," she told him.

"Looks like road rash." He reached beneath the car, then came up with her glasses and handed them to her. "I'm sorry. I wanted you out of the way of those bullets."

Everything came into focus as she put her glasses back on—Buck pulling his gun from beneath his jacket, the V-shaped cut on his cheekbone, the heated, worried look in his eyes that warred with the grim set of his mouth. "Don't you dare apologize to me. You saved me." She touched the stream of blood on his cheek. "A half inch higher and you could have lost your eye."

He shook his head at her concern and raised his head to glance through the shattered windows of her car. "I need you to stay put. I'm going to check it out."

When he pushed to his feet, Chelsea locked a two-fisted grip on his forearm, keeping him down at her level on this side of the car. "You can't go out there. We don't even know if there was more than one shooter."

"I only heard one."

She barely paused for breath. "Did Gordy get pissed off because I didn't want him hitting on me?"

"He was hitting on you—?"

"Did we get caught in the crossfire of a gang fight? What kind of cases are you working on right now? Is there a disgruntled husband who doesn't want you taking pictures of his affair? Did you run a background check on some thug for KCPD?"

"It could be related to one of the cases I'm working, but…" He glanced down at the picture in her lap that had gotten wadded between them. "I don't like the timing."

He thought this was about *her*?

Stop what you're doing. Or someone will get hurt.

She unfolded the picture and smoothed it against her thigh. "I wish I knew what this meant."

"So do I." He squeezed her shoulder, drawing her attention back up to him. "Right now, I need you to stay put. Keep the wheel and the frame of the car between you and that alley."

She scooted over slightly to align her back with the wheel so no stray shots could ricochet under the car and hit her. "Wait." She grabbed his arm again. "You're going across the street where the shots came from?"

"I am. I've already lost the shooter, but I need to at least get a sense of what happened. See if he left tire tracks or footprints or shell casings. With this weather, we might get lucky." He pulled his arm through her grip until he could turn his hand and lace his gloved fingers together with hers. "But I can't do that if I don't know you're safe."

"What about me knowing *you're* safe?"

"Who has experience with this kind of thing?"

Chelsea reluctantly released him. "The veteran cop." She was the computer geek, the research guru. A desk jockey. He was the man of action who went out into the world and took care of business. She sidled up against the wheel. "Right. I'll stay here. Don't worry about me."

"Can't promise that, sweetheart." His big hand came up to cup her cheek, and Chelsea couldn't help but turn her face into the cool leather of his palm. He was the rock-solid anchor in her blithering mess of a world right now. She needed to get her act together so she wouldn't distract him with worry, and to let him do his job. "Yell if you see or hear anything that scares you."

She tilted her gaze to meet his. "I'll call 911 and report shots fired. Go. Be safe."

His fingers tightened on her scalp and the side of her neck, and he pulled her slightly forward as his mouth descended toward hers. But even as her lips parted in anticipation of his reassuring touch there, he altered course and pressed a kiss to her forehead. His lips were firm. They lingered long enough to feel his warm exhale caressing her skin. There was a gentle pressure. Then a firmer press of his mouth that excited her pulse yet proved ultimately frustrating as he pulled away before she could even put a name to what she was feeling. The stubble of his beard caught a few strands of her hair, and he freed them and smoothed them behind her ear before releasing her entirely. "Stay put."

And then he was gone. She heard his footsteps crunching the loose gravel of the parking lot. She heard the swish of a vehicle driving through the slush on the street. There was a token honk, Buck shouting something to the driver, then more footsteps, until the city around her fell relatively silent again. She couldn't turn and watch Buck's progress or ensure his safety without endangering her own. She did peek beneath the car and saw that both tires on the opposite side had gone flat, tilting the vehicle at an angle that prevented her from seeing across the street unless she moved from the position where she'd promised to stay.

Sliding her curiosity about the shooting, her concern for Buck and all the questions she had about that chaste kiss to the back of her mind, she tugged off her glove and dialed 911 to make the report. By the time she was calling Vinnie to warn him to stay inside and not panic when a bunch of flashing lights and police cars appeared outside his apartment and bar, she was calculating permutations of video footage from the security camera in the parking lot and the one over the bar's front door to keep her from obeying the instinct to go after Buck so that he wasn't alone against whatever enemy she'd apparently pissed off. Once she was assured Vinnie was safe, she hung up and called Lexi Callahan—her supervisor and best friend from the crime lab, who now lived with her fiancé, KCPD Officer Aiden Murphy, and his K-9 partner, Blue.

She wasn't surprised to hear Aiden's groggy voice answer since it was so late. "'Lo?"

"Aiden? It's Chelsea."

"What time is it?" he grumbled, no doubt checking his clock. "You okay?"

She hugged her knees up to her chest, forcing herself to stay put, even as she strained to hear any sign of Buck returning to her. "Somebody shot at me at the Sin City Bar."

Aiden cursed, and she heard his K-9 partner, Blue, woof in response as both cop and dog went on alert. "What the hell are you doing there? Is the shooter still around? Did your car break down? Are you hurt? Are the police there?"

"Shooter? What's going on? Is she all right?" She

heard Lexi in the background, asking for an explanation before demanding, "Put her on speaker phone."

"Get up, boy. We need to go to work." Chelsea heard the change in Aiden's voice and knew both her friends were listening now.

She answered the questions she could. "He drove off on a motorcycle. I'm fine, but my car is toast. KCPD is on their way. I could use a couple of friendly faces and some help from the crime lab, though."

"You know I love you like a sister, Chels, but you don't always make sense," Aiden said. From the sounds in the background, Chelsea suspected both her friends were throwing on clothes. "If there's an officer there, put him on the phone."

"They're not here yet," she explained, looking around and realizing just how small and insignificant her perspective was, hunched on the ground in the big parking lot, surrounded by two-story or higher buildings on every side of her. "I get that this isn't the safest part of town. But someone I care about is here, so I am, too."

"Talk to her. I'll get Blue ready." Aiden handed the conversation off to Lexi.

"Chelsea? What's going on?"

As comforting as it was to hear her best friend's voice, she needed the crime lab supervisor more. "Bring your kit."

"Always do. I'll call in the team to help process whatever we need to at the scene." Her voice faded at the end of the sentence. She'd probably set the phone down to tie her shoes or something that required both hands. But that didn't stop the conversation. "You told Aiden something about gunshots? Are you okay?"

"I scraped my elbow. And Buck's cheek is bleeding. I don't know if he got grazed by a bullet or cut by the flying glass."

"Buck's with you? Good. I'll let Aiden know so he'll stop freaking out."

"I'm not freaking—"

"Your shirt's on inside out," Lexi challenged him. When Lexi turned her attention back to the phone, she sounded calm and supportive. "I'll get this rescue squad straightened out, Chels, and we'll leave in a few minutes. Do you have someplace safe where you can wait for us?"

"I'll be wherever Buck is. Probably inside the bar."

"Good. We're on our way."

"Lexi?"

"Yeah?"

"Buck kissed me."

"Are you two on a date?" The timbre of Lexi's voice suddenly changed, and Chelsea knew she'd taken the call off speaker. "Why the hell would he take you to Sin City?"

"He didn't. I called him. He wouldn't leave me." Chelsea dared a peek around the front fender to see if Buck was on his way back yet. Still no sign of him. It was as if the darkness of the alley had swallowed him up and taken him from her. "We were working on our project. Then he walked me to my car and the shooting started and he threw me to the ground. When it was over, he kissed me." She slid back to her hiding place against the wheel. "On the forehead. I thought he was going to give me a real kiss, but…"

"But what?"

Chelsea's breath rushed out on a frustrated sigh.

"Isn't that how you kiss a little girl? Or your daughter? I've never thought about him like he was my father. I'm not sure *how* I was thinking about him before tonight. But I don't want him kissing my forehead." She remembered other details besides the noise and the flying glass. "Lexi, he grabbed me, and I didn't have a panic attack. It wasn't like it was with Dennis at all. I felt safe with Buck touching me. It even felt…exciting. What do you think that means?"

"That you're comfortable with him. That you trust him."

"Of course, I trust him." She knew that. But with her past trauma and relationship history, or lack thereof, didn't it have to mean something more? "I don't understand him. How do I figure out a man?"

Lexi let out a breathy *whew*. "Priorities, Chelsea. We'll talk about this when I get there. Okay? We're just glad you're not alone."

"Me, too. Hurry. Buck went over to where the shooter was. He needs backup."

Aiden must have leaned in beside Lexi to finish up the call. "Backup's on the way. Love ya, kiddo."

Lexi added, "Blue's looking forward to seeing you in a few minutes."

Blue might be a specially trained police officer, but the Belgian Malinois was more like a comfort dog to Chelsea. "Believe me, I'm looking forward to seeing him, too. Bye."

Those two were so good for each other, and they made a formidable team—the criminalist and the cop. Lexi and Aiden had been friends for far too long before they figured out what everyone around them could see—that they were in love with each other. Of course,

Lexi being attacked at a crime scene she'd been working, and Aiden thinking he was going to lose her, had sped the awakening of their feelings. Chelsea couldn't wait to stand up as Lexi's maid of honor when they got married over the Christmas holiday. But right now, she needed her friends around her—her best friend, Lexi, the cop she was engaged to, and Aiden's partner, Blue.

Chelsea jerked at the sound of footsteps running across the parking lot. With her thumb hovering over her phone screen, ready to press 911, she backed against the tire and held her breath.

"Chels?"

When she heard Buck's deep voice, she cleared her phone, stuffed it into her coat pocket and scrambled to her feet. Her boots crunched over broken glass as he came around the corner and she launched herself at his chest. He caught her squarely against him with one arm as she hugged him tight around the waist. "I wasn't sure you'd stay put."

"I wasn't, either," she confessed. "You were gone so long," she said against the piney, leathery scent that was all Buck. "I had time to make three phone calls. What did you find?" Although her fingers still clung to the sides of his jacket, she pulled back the moment she felt his grip around her ease and tipped her chin to meet his steady brown gaze.

"He's long gone, as I suspected." Buck unzipped his jacket to holster his weapon. "He went out the back end of the alley and turned right at the next street. I followed his tracks through the snow until he hit the cleared pavement. He's definitely on a motorcycle. I tried to preserve the tire tread marks as best I could before they melt. But he policed his brass. I couldn't get a make on what he was shooting."

Chelsea had worked at the lab long enough to know a little about weapons. "Could it have been a revolver? They don't eject shell casings."

"Too many bullets fired. It had to be a semiautomatic with a magazine." Buck flattened his hand over hers against his chest. "I'll let your friends at the crime lab do a more thorough search. Right now, I want to get you inside."

"Will you let me look at that cut now? The police are on their way. Vinnie is coming downstairs to let us in. He said he didn't hear the shots because he had the TV up loud. I also called Lexi and Aiden, and they're on their way. Maybe Blue could pick up the shooter's trail." She knew Buck had met Aiden Murphy's K-9 partner. "Tracking isn't Blue's specialty. But he's a natural at so many things. I like Blue. If he's not working, he lets me pet him. I'm not a very good friend. I keep waking people up in the middle of the night."

"Hey." He cupped her jaw and pressed his thumb to her lips to quiet her. "Take a breath and stop rambling, Chels. You're all right."

"Am I rambling?" she questioned against his glove.

His bulldog expression softened, but he didn't quite smile. "It's the adrenaline working its way through your system. You're okay." Her bottom lip stuck to his thumb for a split second, then snapped back as he pulled away. She felt that little tug of an unintended caress shoot through her like an electric current. What was it about Robert Buckner's touch that had her thinking about getting closer instead of screaming in panic and lashing out or running for the hills? He laced his fingers with hers and pulled her along beside him as he inspected the damage to her car. The windshield and driver's-side window had been shot out. And the side facing the alley had at least nine bullet holes, including the shots that had taken out the tires. "Can't say the same for your car, though. Please tell me you have insurance."

Such destruction. She gripped his hand between both of hers and nodded. "I can't imagine what I've done to make someone so angry with me. Except for work, I pretty much keep to myself."

"There were plenty of people at the bar tonight," Buck pointed out, pulling her into step beside him. "And the residents of this neighborhood are notorious for clinging to the shadows. Then there's Dennis Hunt's trial coming up. I'm guessing you've been talking to attorneys? Giving depositions?" He squeezed her hand. "Even if you're minding your own business, that doesn't mean someone else out there isn't aware of you and what you're up to."

Chelsea stopped, thinking through all the possibilities he'd laid out. "That's not very reassuring."

"I'm not trying to be reassuring. I'm being realistic." He faced her and rubbed his free hand up and down her arm. "I know you're laser-focused on your computer screen and the research you do, and that's a legit talent not all of us have. But I'd feel better if you looked up every now and then and took notice of what's going on around you."

She turned her head toward the sound of sirens in the distance and saw Vinnie sticking his head out the bar's front door. "Ladybug?" The old man was tying a plaid robe on over his pajamas. He looked paler than he had earlier. "You okay?"

Buck answered for them. "The shooter made the point he wanted, and he isn't coming back. All the same, I'd rather be inside. Away from the door and windows." He nodded to Vinnie. "You, too, sir."

When they walked around the hood of her car, Chelsea glanced through the gaping hole that had once been her windshield and saw the two small round burn spots in the driver's seat. She couldn't help but raise her hand to her heart. Two bullet holes that would have been in her chest instead of the upholstery if she'd been sitting there. "I really ticked someone off." She swayed a little, colliding with the solid bulk of Buck's body. "That's… I would have been… If you weren't…"

Buck's arm moved around her waist, pulling her away from the disturbing sight. Once they were inside the bar, he led Chelsea over to one of the barstools and spoke to Vinnie. "Can you turn on all the lights? Maybe crank the heat? Her clothes are soaked through."

"Of course." Vinnie paused to squeeze Chelsea's hand before shuffling around the bar. "I'll put on a fresh pot of coffee. Set out a tray of mugs so folks can help themselves. I'll bring a blanket down, too."

Buck thanked him and helped slip Chelsea's backpack off her shoulder. "I'll go out front and wait for the police. You'll be okay by yourself for a few minutes?"

He thought she was going to sit here and stew or mope or tremble with fear while other people took care of her? Outside, where bullets had been flying, she'd deferred to Buck's expertise. But now she was in her element.

"I'll be fine," she assured him. She tossed her ruined coat over a stool. Then she unzipped her bag and pulled out her laptop. Nothing inside appeared to be damaged. "I can tap into the video feed from Vinnie's security cameras." She felt stronger, useful, more in control of her own fate, when she dove into her technical world. "I don't know if the camera can see all the way across the street, but maybe I can capture footage from earlier tonight in the parking lot when he left that note on the windshield." As she typed in the password to Vinnie's security system, she realized Buck was leaning his elbow against the bar beside her, watching her work. And he was smiling. Someone had tried to kill them tonight—or at least do a damn fine job of scaring them—and Buck was smiling. At her. "What?"

He palmed the back of her head and pulled her toward him to press a kiss to her temple, right above her glasses. "That's my girl. You never give up the fight, do you. Just remember to look up every now and then."

Then he was striding out the door to meet the officers in the black-and-white cruisers pulling into the parking lot.

His girl? What exactly did Buck mean by that?

Was that a *Way to go, kid*? Or an *I find your stubborn determination hot*?

And why did the answer matter so much to her?

Chapter Five

Chelsea twisted on the barstool, working the kinks in her back before she readjusted the blanket wrapped around her damp sweater and blouse. She took her glasses off and set them on the bar beside her laptop. She pinched her thumb and index finger together at the bridge of her nose and pushed them outward across her eyebrows, massaging the tension formed by a lethal combination of eyestrain and fatigue that had coiled into a massive headache. Vinnie sat in the first booth, leaning against the wall and snoring. Envious of her friend's ability to slough off the stress of the night and sleep, she stared blankly at the screen. She was exhausted, but her brain wouldn't shut down until she understood why she'd been threatened and why someone had shot at her and Buck tonight.

Chelsea had already given her statement to the police. Buck and Aiden were finishing up with the officers outside.

When the bell over the bar's front door jingled, she grabbed her glasses and twisted around as quickly as her stiff back could manage, then sighed in disappointment as Lexi and two of Chelsea's other coworkers, Shane Duvall and Jackson Dobbs, walked in. Not that she wasn't grateful to see her friends, but when was Buck coming back?

And why did it feel like a part of her couldn't settle until she had him in her sights again?

Buck couldn't exactly take the lead on this investigation since he was no longer with KCPD. But he was an honored veteran of the department, and a consultant with the crime lab. Plus, she supposed his old-school instincts died hard. They would value his input into the investigation. He'd told her to look up from her computer more often, but every time she did, he wasn't there. And every time he wasn't, she battled a surge of disappointment. Maybe he was avoiding her. She really had caused him a lot of trouble tonight.

"Hey, guys," she greeted them. She could tell by the weary look on their faces that they were done for the night—from Jackson scrubbing his fingers over the late-night stubble of his beard, to Lexi stifling a yawn that seemed to go on forever behind her hand. All three wore their CSI vests, but since none of them carried their kits, she assumed they were done processing the scene and had stowed any evidence they'd found in the CSIU van for processing at the lab.

Chelsea summoned a tired smile. "Sorry to call you out so late. I owe you all a big favor."

"No, you don't." She traded a hug with Shane. "I'd like to say we're just doing our job," the resident single dad of the group assured her. "But when it happens to one of us, you know we're going to help out. Lexi gelled us into a team again—a family—despite a couple of bad eggs who tried to turn the crime lab into their own personal hunting ground. We're not going to let anyone divide our loyalties or make us hide away in our isolated cubicles again."

"What he said." Chelsea tilted her gaze up—way up—to meet Jackson's ice-gray eyes. His stoic demeanor was a well-practiced deterrent to most people striking up conversations and getting close to him.

But Chelsea suspected there was a true heart inside the taciturn beast and counted him among her friends. Besides, she was a hugger from way back. She slipped her arms around Jackson's waist and gave him a quick squeeze. "Thank you. Did you find anything useful?"

Jackson tucked the blanket back around her shoulders as she released him, and she interpreted the gesture as his way of expressing that he cared, too. "Pulled two slugs from your car—9 mm. Glock or SIG Sauer. Possibly a Walther Q5." She suspected that Jackson, as the lab's resident expert in weaponry, would have the gun's make narrowed down in no time. "Found trace on one. The roundish doughnut shape reminds me of lipstick. Only, it's clear."

"Lip prints can be like fingerprints if we can pull a full impression," Lexi added. "Not that we keep those on file. But we can compare striations and scarring to pictures, and certainly try to match the impression to any suspects KCPD might bring in."

"Sounds like a long shot." Chelsea frowned. "You think the shooter kissed the bullet before loading his gun? That's a little creepy."

Lexi shrugged. "He could have held it in his mouth while he was loading the magazine." She briefly stuck her finger between her lips to demonstrate how the mark could have been made. "At the very least, we should be able to identify the substance."

"And hope we can find a perp who puts the same stuff on his or her lips?"

"His," Lexi confirmed. "I found a big boot print near the spot where Buck said the shooter had parked his bike. Unless you have a giant woman mad at you?"

"Not that I know of." Chelsea rolled her eyes. "Buck seems to think I've got more than one guy who might have it in for me."

"He's feeding Aiden a list. Dennis Hunt. A motorcycle gang? Some preppie dude in here with a hooker? Someone involved in this side job you're doing for Buck?" Lexi reached out to squeeze Chelsea's hand. "Girl, you are the sweetest, smartest, most helpful woman I know—but you're gonna give me a heart attack."

Didn't that sound familiar? Chelsea glanced toward the door. Still no sign of Buck. "I don't mean to worry anyone."

The squeeze turned into another hug. "I know you don't. But I'm not a big fan of people shooting at my friends." She pulled away with a gentle admonishment. "Let us do our job and find this guy, and you watch your back."

"I can help," Chelsea reminded them. The crime lab worked as a team, and she was part of that team.

Shane answered this time. "We'll run ballistics, see if we can match it to any weapon used in a previous crime. Also, our shooter has skills, or else he's damn lucky. Even though Buck's truck was parked next to yours, every shot went into your car. His wasn't even scratched. There were no strays I could find, and neither of you were hit."

Chelsea understood where he was going with his

observation. "I can run a database search to check gun clubs, ex-military, former cops—anyone who might have that kind of proficiency with a handgun in the area." Her friends were the experts at the crime scene who found the facts, and she was the one who found out the details surrounding those facts.

Lexi tucked her golden-brown hair behind her ears, then poured herself a mug of coffee from the pot on the bar. "I also made impressions of the tire tracks Buck preserved. Once we source it, we'll need to generate a list of everyone who owns that model of motorcycle. Maybe we'll get lucky and discover they belong to a customized bike, to make our list shorter."

And maybe they'd be factory-issue, with hundreds of that model of motorcycle in the KC area alone. But Chelsea appreciated Lexi's optimism.

"I can run those searches later." Chelsea turned to her laptop and pulled up a couple of dark, blurry pictures. "In the meantime, I've cleaned up the images with the equipment I have here. I can do better at the lab. But this is what I've got from the parking lot and the alley across the street."

Lexi, Shane and Jackson all leaned in to study the screen grab of the back of a man with a dark covering over his head, holding up Chelsea's windshield wiper to place the note without ever facing the camera. Besides the falling snow that dotted the image, he wore a backpack and bent over the hood of her car, further distorting his silhouette, making it difficult to get an accurate assessment of his build or height. The second image was even grainier because of the later hour and longer distance from the camera above the bar's front door. Although the image showed the man's arms sticking out from the shadows in the alley, the only clear part of the picture was the fiery flash from the barrel of the gun as he shot across the street. The man himself was a blob of darkness within the shadows. There was barely a slash of chin visible, captured by the momentary burst of light from the gun's tiny explosion. A white male, judging by the size and squareness of that chin. That narrowed down the pool of suspects to, oh, say, half of Kansas City.

Jackson pointed to a tiny reflection of light that was barely a glow beside the blob's dark form. "License plate?"

There were no discernible details from that angle and distance, but the shape was rectangular. Chelsea nodded. "The proportion is the right size to be a motorcycle tag. It'd take a miracle to get a number off that."

"I know someone who works miracles on a daily basis," Lexi praised her. "Could you get us more detail if you use your setup at the lab? If you can't get a plate number or anything through facial recognition, maybe you can get a brand name off that backpack in the other picture."

"Or make of the gun?" Shane suggested.

"I'll try." Chelsea clicked on her email and attached the pictures to send them to her work email address.

"We've got your car up on a tow truck," Shane explained. "We'll take it to the lab. Run the whole thing for prints or other trace. Hopefully, the weather didn't wash away everything." He nodded to Lexi. "I've also got the note from the car you bagged."

"We'll start processing first thing in the morning," Lexi insisted, her green eyes sliding over to Chelsea. "I want to catch this guy. If this attack has anything to do with one of our cases, or if threatening Chelsea is an attempt to dissuade her from testifying against Dennis, I want to know about it ASAP and put a stop to it."

"You got it, boss." Shane smiled at Chelsea. "Take care."

Jackson's eyes met hers and he nodded before they both headed to the door. If Chelsea had more energy, she'd be speculating about what had happened to Jackson to make him so reticent to say much or share his emotions. She sometimes wondered if he even had a sense of humor. But she was too tired right now to use up mental energy on the ongoing mystery of Jackson Dobbs. The man knew his weapons, none of the few words he'd ever said to her had been unkind, and though he was big and muscular, he had never once used that brawn to intimidate her or anyone else at the lab. She was glad that he was on her team, and not working against them.

"Good night, guys," she called after them. "Thanks!"

With a friendly wave from Shane, the two men disappeared into the night. Chelsea was left with two blurry images, her best friend and the rattle of Vinnie's soft snoring filling the otherwise quiet bar.

Lexi pulled out the stool beside Chelsea's and sat. She picked up her mug of coffee and wrapped her fingers around it, savoring its warmth rather than the caffeine. "Do you have any idea what that note means? 'Stop what you're doing, or someone will get hurt'?"

"I assume it's something related to work." Chelsea poured a shot of cream into her own mug and stirred it around, watching the cloud dissipate into the dark liquid, reminding her of the light and dark contrasts in Buck's closely cropped hair. "I put a troll bot on my search program, to see if I've pinged on someone who thinks I'm tracking them online. I have legitimate access to almost every database, so I shouldn't have thrown up any alarms on the cases I've been working." She licked the spoon, then set both the mug and utensil aside to meet Lexi's querying expression. "The infosec on my laptop is all in place, and my portable hot spot gives my Wi-Fi connection a limited range. The security with my lab setup is even more state-of-the-art, so if this is an online thing, the guy has some mad hacking skills to track me down through my computers."

Lexi translated Chelsea's explanation into simpler terms. "You're reviewing the work you've been doing online to see if you've piqued anyone's interest?"

Chelsea grinned at the oversimplification. "No hits yet, but I'll let the tracer run for a while. I've got years of research history on countless cases to go through."

"Maybe not. You didn't get a threat until tonight. Chances are, if this guy is someone you tagged online, it didn't happen until recently. You should include the research you're doing for Buck, too. Let's do a meeting tomorrow so you can brief me on what you've uncovered for him. I want to know all the possibilities of where this threat came from. We have forensic evidence, but we need a way to put it into context and make sense of it." Lexi inhaled the steam from her coffee, sighed as if saying good-night to the fragrant brew, then set it on the bar beside Chelsea's mug. "In the meantime, I'll ask Aiden to contact the detectives who put together the case against Dennis so that they can find out where he's been tonight. Maybe this attack isn't tech-related at all. The creep's out on bail. I don't know if Dennis is a marksman, but he could have hired someone to shoot at you. Maybe this is his last-ditch effort to scare you out of testifying against him."

"He won't," Chelsea assured her. She tilted her gaze to Lexi, needing the reassurance that they were in this trial together. "We're a team against him, right? All the women he harassed at the crime lab while he was our supervisor are appearing as witnesses."

"Of course. But the charges you're testifying to are the crimes that could get him serious prison time if convicted. Assault. Extortion. Tampering with evidence. He sees you as the biggest threat. Without you, he might get time served and probation. Your testimony could get him years in Jefferson City."

"That's what I want. Let him make friends with Randy Leighton while he's inside. Those two deserve each other."

Lexi reached over to squeeze Chelsea's hand. "Leighton was your abuser when you were in foster care?"

Chelsea had imagined multiple versions of her justice-served scenario in her head. "I want all the men who ever hurt me to do each other in so I can get on with my life and find one who doesn't look at me as if I'm easy prey he can use for whatever game he wants to play." She rolled her eyes and shook her head. "Not that I condone murder. But my therapist says using my imagination like that is a good outlet for stress, and it can help reduce the frequency and severity of my PTSD episodes. If I envision being strong and seeing justice served, then I will be strong." Chelsea shrugged. "Something like that."

"Sounds like good advice to me." Lexi paused the heart-to-heart for a moment to be her boss. "I see the changes in you from that first day Mac hired you at the lab. You're more social, more confident. Dennis was an unfortunate setback for a lot of us. We'll get this trial behind you, and you'll prove to any doubters that you aren't someone to mess with."

"You don't think I'll forever be known as the 'nerdy nutcase'?" It was a phrase Dennis had used more than once when he'd been at the crime lab. "Is there really a man out there who values me? Maybe even thinks I'm kind of cute?"

Back in friend mode, Lexi leaned in and clasped both of Chelsea's hands. "That man is out there, Chels. He'll find you, and the things that Leighton and Dennis did will fade into an unpleasant memory. You have to be ready for the opportunity when it comes and fight for it. Look at Aiden and me. A couple of workaholics who never realized how much we meant to each other until we stopped saving the world for two seconds and listened to our hearts." She pulled away, smiling with a renewed energy. "Speaking of romance, let's talk about the other issue you mentioned on the phone."

"What's that?"

"Buck." Lexi arched an eyebrow, daring Chelsea to play dumb about all the questions she'd asked earlier. "Former KCPD cop turned successful businessman. Smart. Fit. Good-looking in that manly-man way that makes you think of the hero's mentor or superior officer in those action movies Aiden and I love to watch. A little too serious for my taste, but a potentially stellar kisser since you made a point of mentioning that."

She'd described Buck to a tee—and pretty much summed up Chelsea's confusion about exactly what kind of relationship she had with him.

Chelsea pointed to her forehead. "This is where he

kissed me. Hardly the romantic subplot to one of those movies. I think I'm more of the spunky sidekick. Important to the plot, but not to the happy ending."

Lexi was sticking with her action movie analogy. "Well, it's hardly fair to judge how he kisses when bullets are flying."

"The bullets had stopped before he kissed me. Or pseudo-kissed me. Or sidekick-kissed me." She turned to her computer to shut it down and was startled to see her screensaver dotted with various icons. Where were the images her team had just been analyzing? "Where did my pictures go?" A self-conscious alarm buzzed through her veins as she opened the Trash and searched her Pictures file. They weren't in her downloads, either. She opened her Search screen, then realized she hadn't named the images of the man at her car and in the alleyway. She pressed her palms to either side of her head and tried to remember her actions from a few minutes earlier. Had she saved them into a wrong file? Could she recall any of the numeric code that they would default to? "What did I do?"

"What's wrong?"

She typed in a Recent files command, but there was nothing there. "I lost those pictures on my screen. The shooter. The license plate. I don't remember closing them out after I emailed them." She didn't make mistakes like that. She missed seeing men in alleys, was bamboozled by social cues, and sometimes tripped over her own feet. But she didn't make mistakes with her computer. "My brain is tired, and I'm distracted by man things I don't understand. I must have deleted those screen grabs from Vinnie's security feed." She reopened her email. The attachments were there, but they opened up with an error message. No pictures.

She felt Lexi's hand at her back, offering her a supportive hug. "We have other evidence to work with."

Panic warred with fatigue as Chelsea gestured to the empty screen. "But this is my contribution to the case. This is how I help you guys."

Lexi's hug tightened. "You can download the video again tomorrow and work with it when your mind is fresh."

Exhaling a sigh of frustration, Chelsea shut down her computer, irritated with herself for losing the evidence. "It's an amateur move. Makes me feel like a victim, not a criminalist."

"You *are* the victim tonight," Lexi gently pointed out. "You had a hell of a scare. Don't beat yourself up for being human like the rest of us." Lexi picked up Chelsea's backpack and unzipped the laptop compartment. "I know you. When you're feeling more like yourself again, you'll put on that brainiac cap of yours and fix this glitch like it was nothing." Once Chelsea had stuffed her equipment inside the bag, a grin teased Lexi's tired expression. "Of course, maybe sleep isn't what you need. Maybe you need a little one-on-one session with the suave, sexy mentor of the movie."

"Lexi!" Chelsea glanced quickly around them, making sure no one had overheard what her friend was intimating. "Buck and I aren't like that. I don't think he sees me as…dating material."

Lexi snorted her disagreement. "You're a ridiculously smart, funny, beautiful woman and you have the biggest heart of anyone I've ever known. Buck is no idiot. Of course, he sees that."

"I do have a crush on him," she confessed. "Have you felt the biceps on that man? He's the solid and dependable I've never had in my life." She pointed to the bottles above the bar. "His eyes are the color of that top-shelf whiskey, but they rarely smile. I'm impulsive and he watches and waits and makes a decision before he acts. He's established and mature, down-to-earth—none of the things anyone ever says about me. He belongs with someone who's polished and classy and comes from the right background, someone who's a little less flaky and a lot less trouble than I am."

"Did he say that? I'll sic Blue on him."

Chelsea shook her head. "We don't have conversations like that."

"Maybe you should."

"Why?"

"Because you wanted to have this conversation with me. You want to know where you stand with him. You're disappointed that he didn't flat-out kiss you like a man kisses a woman." Lexi tilted her head with a wry expression. "But is that your ego's opinion? Or your heart's? Maybe you should figure out how you feel about him first. Then we'll worry about his feelings for you."

"I love your logic." Chelsea hugged Lexi again. "Thanks for being my friend and talking me out of the mess inside my head." She pulled away when she heard the bell jingling over the door.

Vinnie startled awake. He sat up straight in his booth and shouted, "We're closed!"

"It's okay, Vinnie." Chelsea hurried over to reassure him by touching his arm and stealing his forgotten coffee mug away. She'd been startled by the jangling noise, too, but instead of alarm, her reaction was pure relief tinged with a rush of anticipation at seeing Buck, Aiden and Blue walk in. Clutching the blanket to her like a shawl, Chelsea returned to the bar to drop the mug into the sink. "Well?" she asked, turning her full attention to the male trio.

"All clear outside," Aiden announced, unhooking Blue's leash.

Chelsea's smile stretched the tired muscles on her face as Aiden's Belgian Malinois partner spotted Chelsea and trotted over to her. "There's my good boy." Blue was one male she understood. He rolled over on the floor at her feet, demanding a tummy rub. Chelsea knelt beside the muscular dog and happily obliged, loving how his tongue lolled out of his mouth, making him look as though he was smiling at her touch. She glanced up at Aiden, who had crossed to Lexi to slide an arm around her waist. "Is it all right if I give him a treat?"

"You spoil my dog, Chels." But he nodded, and she dug a treat from one of the pockets of her backpack. "He's supposed to be a tough guy."

"He *is* a tough guy when he's on the job." Blue eagerly sat up to accept the crunchy treat, then trotted off to lie down and enjoy his reward. "But he's a teddy bear with me."

Not unlike Buck. Chelsea felt her cheeks warm as she looked up at the older man pouring himself a mug of coffee at the bar. Had she just compared Buck to the dog? While she'd always thought dogs were about the finest, most loyal life forms on the planet, she doubted Buck—or maybe any man—would see that as much of a compliment.

Buck swallowed a drink of the strong brew, then turned to face her. She quickly lowered her gaze to his mug. "I can't imagine what your stomach lining and heart rate must be like. How many cups of coffee have you had tonight?" Those careworn lines beside his eyes deepened a fraction. She knew Buck was divorced, and she wondered if he had anyone in his life who took care of him when he stayed up late working, or who comforted him when he despaired over ever finding his son again. She must have been staring a little too long because his eyebrows arched with an unspoken question. Was he as alone against the world as she sometimes felt? Chelsea shook off her wandering thoughts and plucked the mug from his fingers. "I'm cutting you off."

"You can't separate a man from his caffeine at this hour."

"I just did." She set the mug on the bar before reaching up to touch the dried blood on his cheek. "Did anyone look at your cut yet? We've got a first aid kit here." She patted the top of the nearest barstool before setting aside the blanket and hurrying behind the bar. "Sit." He was still standing there when she returned with the first aid kit. "Please?"

He opened his mouth as if to protest being babied, but at her soft plea for cooperation, he reluctantly sat. Chelsea set the kit on the bar and pulled out an alcohol wipe and ripped open the package. She nudged his knee to one side and stepped between his thighs before pulling her glasses down her nose to study the injury in sharper detail with her nearsighted eyes.

Fortunately, the dried blood had stanched the wound, but as she gently dabbed at the injury, it opened up again, revealing a small but wide triangular gash. "You probably need a stitch or two. Or some of that glue to seal it so it doesn't scar." After cleaning the wound, she reached for Buck's hand and pushed it up to hold the gauze against his cheek, keeping the pressure there while she turned to retrieve antibiotic ointment and a butterfly bandage. Although her distance vision was out of focus with her glasses perched on the end of her nose, she was vaguely aware of Lexi gently elbowing Aiden in the side, and her friend smiling as she watched Chelsea work.

Whatever. She already felt a little useless with all the trouble she'd caused her friends tonight. But if she could do this one small thing for Buck, she would. She leaned in to pinch the wound together and seal it with the bandage. Standing this close, she could smell the piney scent of Buck's aftershave or bodywash, along with the muskier scent that was Buck himself. She could also make out the individual hairs of his beard stubble. They were mostly brown, mixed with a few that were a darker sable shade, and more that were silver, truly driving home the salt-and-pepper design reflected in his short hair. Then she raised her gaze a fraction higher and saw those whiskey-brown eyes anchored onto hers, watching her as intently as she studied the compelling landscape of his face. "I…um…"

"I'm fine," he murmured in that deep voice that resonated in her ears. "Thank you."

His hands had settled lightly at her waist, and she realized she was standing in the vee of his legs, leaning in closely enough to feel the heat radiating off his body, to smell the coffee on his breath. No wonder Lexi was bemused by her Florence Nightingale routine. For a woman who wasn't sure what was going on between her and Buck, she was certainly making herself at home in his personal space. Feeling the blush heating her cheeks, Chelsea pushed her glasses onto the bridge of her nose to blur all those masculine details, and stepped away to clean up the mess she'd made. "You're welcome. Did you find anything?" she asked, skirting around the back of the bar to use the trash and put the first aid kit away. "I hope so, because I lost the pictures from the security footage."

"Lost them?"

Chelsea waved aside Buck's question. "They have to be on my computer somewhere. I'll look for them when I can focus in a little better."

She was still hovering behind the bar, filling the sink with hot, sudsy water to wash the coffee mugs when Aiden asked, "Can you think of anyone who wants to hurt you?"

"Murph, we've already been over this," Buck warned. "Give her a break."

Aiden wasn't intimidated. "I need to hear it from her."

Buck's defense boosted her mood, making it a little easier to discuss the enemies Chelsea had never expected to have. "Besides Dennis?"

Aiden nodded. Along with his partner, Blue, he'd been the one to arrest Dennis at the lab—right after he'd pinned Lexi to the wall and accused her of gunning for his job and setting him up for the charges he was now facing.

Lexi linked her arm through Aiden's and leaned against his shoulder. "Dennis owns a motorcycle. Remember him talking about riding on weekends with his fiancée?"

Chelsea pushed up her sleeves and dipped her hands in the sudsy water. "You think she's still going to marry him after everything he's been accused of?"

"Maybe she's turning a blind eye and standing by her man."

Chelsea handed the first mug to Vinnie, who'd moved in beside her with a dish towel to dry. "There's Gordy Bismarck," he suggested. "He obviously rides a motorcycle, and he was here with his gang buddies tonight."

"Hitting on Chels," Buck pointed out.

"I told him to take a hike." Chelsea directed her answer to Buck. "And later, you did that glaring thing you didn't think I saw. I think we shut him down."

Buck faced her across the bar, looking intimidating without even standing up. "He was drunk. He's got a history of hurting women. And he's got street cred to maintain to allow anyone to tell him no. Especially in front of his buddies. Could be reason enough for him to shoot at us."

Aiden pulled up Gordy's name on his phone and skimmed the information from the KCPD database. "Bismarck's got a record a mile long. Several domestic abuse incidents. None of them involved a gun, though."

Chelsea handed off the next mug. "He could be escalating. Especially with Buck here—maybe he didn't think his fists would be enough to go up against him."

Aiden seemed doubtful. "Could a guy that wasted make clean shots like that?"

"He had plenty of friends here," Buck pointed out. "He could have called in a favor."

"Time out, everyone." Lexi did the logical boss thing by reminding them of the difference between speculation and facts they could corroborate. "Let's consider what evidence we do have first. See if we can identify the gun that goes with those bullets. Find and analyze those images off the camera footage. See if we can pinpoint the type of printer and ink used on that photograph." She squeezed Aiden's hand. "I'll run things from my end at the lab, and you do your thing and follow up on our suspects' alibis. I'll fill in Captain Stockman and Mac." She meant the KCPD officer who oversaw the CSIU, and the veteran criminalist who ran the entire crime lab. "I'll let them coordinate with whoever ends up investigating the shooting. Let's salvage a few hours of sleep tonight, and tackle everything fresh in the morning."

Aiden leaned over to kiss her cheek. "Sounds like a plan. Blue! *Hier!*" He released her as the Belgian Malinois trotted over to his side to get hooked up to his lead.

Lexi extended her hand across the bar to Vinnie. "Mr. Goring, thank you for letting us use your bar. We'll get out of your hair and let you go back to bed."

After Lexi, Aiden and Blue left, Vinnie took the dishrag from Chelsea and nudged her aside. "You get out of here, too, Ladybug. Be safe. I'd hate it if anything happened to you."

He held out his arms and Chelsea walked in for a hug. "Same here."

Vinnie lifted his chin toward Buck. "You're taking her home?"

"Yes, sir."

"Good. You run along, then. I'll finish up here." He watched Chelsea slip into her ruined coat and slide her backpack over her shoulder. "I'm going to close the place for a couple of nights. See you Saturday?"

She felt Buck's hand at the small of her back. "I don't think that's a good—"

"I'll be here."

Like Lexi, Vinnie seemed to think there was something more going on between her and Buck. "Then I expect I'll be seeing you, too?"

"Yep." Without losing touch with her back, he reached over the bar to shake Vinnie's hand. "Keep the coffee fresh. I don't drink on duty."

The two men exchanged a nod. With his gaze swiveling on a constant scan, Buck walked her out to his truck as Vinnie locked up behind them.

"You don't have to play bodyguard for me. I've worked at Sin City on and off for years now. I know these people. I'll be fine."

"It's nonnegotiable, Chels. How many of those times has anyone shot at you before tonight?"

"None."

He opened the passenger door for her to climb in. He filled the opening before she could buckle up, to make his point. "And with your car out of commission, how are you going to get home? Walk by yourself to the bus stop? Do you think a reliable car service is going to come to this part of town on a Saturday night? Even if you rent another car, you risk being the last person in the parking lot again. Who's going to walk you out? Make sure there's not another threat waiting for you?" He nodded toward the bar and Vinnie. "That sweet grandpa figure you love who can't even stand up straight?"

Chelsea couldn't deny that those were the options

she'd been considering. He was turning up the heat inside the truck and pulling out of the parking lot before she answered. "It sounds worse when you say it like that."

"It's not a good situation, no matter how I say it." Buck's chest expanded with a deep breath as he turned toward her home in Independence. "My blood pressure won't tolerate another night like this. You're too important to me—too important to finding Bobby—for me to let you take risks like that when I know damn well I can protect you." He glanced across the front seat as he slowed for a stop light. "It's my job, Chels. Running security ops is a big part of what I do. It's hardwired into my DNA to protect people. I don't handle it well when I fail."

Even though she felt inexplicably hurt to hear him describe protecting her as a job, she also heard the anguish in his tone. What had happened tonight wasn't entirely about her. She reached over to lay her hand over his where it rested on the center console. "You think you failed to protect your son."

Buck laced his fingers with hers. "I should have seen the threat coming—the struggle Bobby was facing. I should have done something different—something more. Even if he didn't want to be part of our family any longer, at least I could have made sure he was safe."

She turned in her seat to face him when he pulled away to put both hands on the wheel and concentrate on his driving. The streets were fairly quiet at this time of the morning, but she could see his eyes were still searching and evaluating every alley and vehicle they passed. "Now you see a clear threat against me, and you intend to do something about it."

"I do."

Chelsea didn't want to read too much into his vow to protect her. But his insistence that he wanted her to be safe filled her with an unfamiliar warmth, a link to some emotion she wasn't sure she could trust. "You have other cases you're working. Paying jobs? I probably can't afford your services."

"I'm not charging you for my help," he snapped. That was probably his fatigue talking, so she didn't take offense at his sharp tone. "God knows I already owe you more than I can ever repay. I'll farm any other jobs out to my team. You're my top priority. I won't make the same mistakes again. I need you to be completely honest with me about anything else that happens. And if there is a tangible threat, then I expect you to do what I say when I say it." His tone barely softened as he looked across at her in the dim glow of light from the dashboard. "Does that make me bossy and overbearing?"

"It is kind of old-school alpha male of you."

"I *am* old-school alpha male."

Chelsea grinned at his determination to be gruff with her. "It's also kind of hot."

"I'm too old to be hot."

"That's bull…" Chelsea summoned the energy to push away from the seat. "Men get better with age. Besides, if beauty is in the eye of the beholder, then so is hotness. And you, Robert Buckner, are…" She quickly glanced away to count the streetlamps they passed. Had she really been about to tell him she thought he was hot? Sexy? Confident in his own skin and masculine in a way that a younger man could never pull off? She cracked her window to let some cooler air into the cab of the truck. "I'm going to stop talking now."

"No, you won't." When she heard him chuckling, she quickly turned to see his face relaxed with a genuine smile.

Surprised by his teasing, Chelsea's breath caught for a moment. Had she ever heard him laugh? Those blunt features were almost handsome when he smiled like that. "I'm trying to say that I've never had anybody like you in my life. Someone so determined to look out for me. I've always had to rely on my own brains and some dumb luck to survive."

The smile instantly faded, and he reached for her hand, pulling it across the center console to rest atop his muscular thigh. "There's nothing dumb about you, sweetheart. Your resourcefulness and caring are mind-boggling." He stroked his thumb over the back of her knuckles, and she felt that simple caress all the way up her arm and deeper inside. "I can honestly say I've never had anybody like you in my life, either. But I *am* in your life. And I will do whatever is necessary to keep you safe."

"Because you need me to help you find your son."

"Because I need you to be safe. Period."

He released her and Chelsea twisted her fingers together in her lap. She'd have to talk to Lexi about what that meant, too.

Chapter Six

"Thanks for the ride." Chelsea's fingers were on the door handle of the truck as Buck pulled into the driveway beside her small, turn-of-the-century house on a fenced-in half acre of land a few blocks north of the historic town square in Independence. She pushed open the door. "See you later."

Buck's hand clamped around her wrist to keep her from climbing out. "I'll walk you in."

"It's literally ten feet from your truck." She dangled her keys in her free hand to show him she was being considerate of his time, not reckless with her own safety. "You can watch me the entire way. The porch light is on. I'll go right in that side door and lock it behind me."

Now that the wintry clouds and flurries had cleared away, moonlight streamed through the windshield, creating shadows beneath the angles on Buck's weary face, but doing nothing to cool the intensity of his dark eyes. "Old-school alpha male, remember? I'm walking you to the door tonight, and I'm picking you up in the morning."

Chelsea smiled at what was turning into a charming private joke between them. "No to you being my full-time taxi service. But if you insist on being a gentleman, and maybe also want to look around inside to make sure everything is as it should be, I wouldn't argue with you."

"I planned to check your home security, anyway."

"Of course, you did." She couldn't say she was offended by his bossy directives, especially after knowing they'd come far too close to dying at Sin City earlier. In fact, it was unexpectedly nice to feel like Buck was taking some of the burden of her crazy life from her shoulders tonight. Chelsea hadn't felt truly safe in the world since the first night her foster father had snuck into her bedroom and stripped her pajama pants off her. With therapy, maturity, a menagerie of pets, strong locks and a few good friends, she'd learned over the years that there were degrees of *safe* that she could feel.

But there was something about Robert Buckner that the little ball of insecurity living deep inside her craved. Despite his bulldog features and brusque demeanor, Buck's presence filled her with a sense of calm. He felt like her safe place, centering her in a way that made her feel as though she could take a deep breath and relax without worrying. He was the first man who grounded her enough to allow her to feel other things. Something more than friendship. A connection. A need. A desire to deepen the bond they shared. And yes, even for a woman who'd been abused as she had, a sexual attraction.

But just because she felt something, it didn't necessarily mean that Buck did, too. "I'm sorry I'm such a burden to you. I don't mean to be—"

"Do not finish that sentence." He held up a warning finger. "What did I say about all these unnecessary apologies? You feel what you feel. I'm always going to be straight with you, Chels. And I want you to be the same with me. If you think I'm being a bully, call me on it. Just know that when I'm in protector mode, I will say or do what I think is necessary to keep you safe."

"I don't think you're a bully," she answered quietly. "I'm not used to anyone looking out for me the way you do. I don't know how to respond to that. Thank you."

"That response works for me." His voice, deep and hushed, skittered along her nerves, and left them tingling with awareness. The finger he'd pointed at her a moment earlier now settled beneath her chin, tilting her face to the moonlight. "You're welcome." Despite the cool light, his eyes warmed as he studied her face. His gaze locked onto hers for an endless moment before sweeping around her hair and cheeks and settling on her lips. Chelsea felt her own temperature rise beneath that heated perusal. Was he thinking about kissing her? His nostrils flared, and she wondered if he was feeling the same curious hunger she was. But he blinked, breaking the mesmerizing spell, and pulled away. "Stay put. I'll come around."

Chelsea exhaled the breath she'd been holding as she watched Buck walk around the hood of his truck. He scanned the length of the driveway from the street to the detached garage and fenced-in backyard before opening her door. "I wasn't aware of the Robert Buckner rules for hitching a ride home."

"They're not my rules," he insisted. He closed his hand around her elbow to help her down off the running board to the driveway. He closed the truck behind them and walked her back along the path he'd taken.

"You've never had a man walk you to your door before?"

"Um…" She'd never actually had any man in her house unless she was hosting a work-related function, like when Aiden, Lexi and Blue had come over for a game night. Or the time she'd babysat Shane Duvall's toddler son. Or a repairman was on the premises for some reason, like the cable guy who'd been here just last week to upgrade the lines into her house after a squirrel had chewed through the junction box on the telephone pole out front. But a man walking her to the door?

"Is that a no?"

He released her when she stepped up onto the porch. "Are you asking about the guys I've dated?"

Since the side porch was no bigger than the size of a vestibule, he waited on the step below her. "I'm asking about any other risks you've been taking when I'm not around."

"How do you think I've been getting inside? All. By. My. Self."

"Smart-ass."

She loved the sound of that low-pitched chuckle, loved that she'd heard Buck laugh more tonight than she had in the past several months she'd known him. It made her feel proud to know that she could elicit those chuckles and smiles—and happy to learn that he wasn't such a hard case that he wouldn't share those responses with her. Chelsea inserted her key into the dead bolt, unable to stop her own smile from forming. "I don't date much," she confessed. "I'm sort of an acquired taste. And I don't, you know—put out—to compensate for being so…" She shrugged, pulling some of the adjectives she'd been called from her memories. "Stuck inside my own head? Eccentric? High-maintenance?"

"In what world are you high-maintenance?" Buck's humor disappeared. He stepped up onto the porch with her, crowding her against the railing. "Let me get this straight. Has somebody said that to you? Demanded you *put out* in exchange for another date?"

Chelsea reached around him to insert her key in the doorknob lock, already hearing the first bark of her dogs and the scrabbling of footsteps running toward the door. "You know how I was when Dennis assaulted me. Total meltdown. Haven't been on a date since. I've got a few hang-ups about intimacy. I keep thinking, with the right man, it will be different. So far—" with the one notable exception standing beside her "—not." One of the cats jumped up onto the window ledge beside the door, and Chelsea tapped the glass and earned an excited meow. Then she shifted her keys to the door-knob. "I've learned that freaking out on a guy is not a big turn-on. But, like I said, I don't date much. So, the whole putting-out/walking-me-to-my-door thing doesn't come up."

Buck pulled her hand away from the door and tugged it to his flank beneath his soft leather jacket. Before she could question what he was doing, he'd folded his arms around her back and pulled her into his chest, swallowing her up in a big bear hug. "What the hell are they teaching young men these days?"

He palmed the back of her neck to tuck her head beneath his chin and Chelsea melted into him. She breathed him in, filling her head with the piney scent of his skin and the earthy leather of his jacket. While he held her tight, she slipped her arms around his waist and latched on, absorbing his strength and heat. Oh, yeah. That needy little ball of insecurity inside her definitely wanted this.

Buck held her close for several seconds, a minute maybe, ignoring the background chorus of dogs and cats raising a ruckus on the other side of the door. His fingers were moving through her hair now, massaging her scalp. Every frayed nerve ending in Chelsea relaxed in his embrace, then reawakened to the scent and feel of man and strength and trust. She fit perfectly beneath his chin, her small breasts softening against his harder chest, his arms cinched securely around her. Her nipples tingled and pricked to attention at the friction between them, triggering a warm heaviness that seemed to slide through her body and gather in the juncture between her thighs. It was a pleasurable sensation, not a reason to panic. She could feel the leather and elastic strap of his shoulder holster crisscrossing his back beneath his coat, but she wasn't alarmed by evidence of a weapon. She kept waiting for that moment when she'd feel trapped, when the press of a man's body would make her uneasy, when she'd fight like a wildcat to free herself. But the moment never came.

It was the second time Buck had taken her into his arms tonight. She felt feminine and sheltered and not at all afraid. The sensation of being held by a man and truly enjoying it was so delicious that Chelsea hummed with a sigh of contentment.

If the fatigue in her body hadn't chosen that very moment to express itself in a noisy yawn, she wondered how long she could have stood in his arms like that— feeling like a normal woman, feeling like part of a couple. Buck's chest expanded with a deep breath, easing some space between them as he untangled his fingers from her hair. Then he pulled away, pressing a familiar kiss to her forehead before ending the embrace.

She tilted her eyes to his. "What was that for?"

"An apology for every man on the planet who didn't treat you with the respect and caring you deserve."

"I thought you didn't like apologies."

"Only when they're unwarranted." He cupped his hand under her chin again. "You are *you*. Brainy, unconventional, whatever. If a man coerces you into changing who you are to suit what he wants, then he's not the guy for you." He released her entirely before twisting the doorknob. He swept his fingers over the locks and strike plate, making sure the door hadn't been tampered with. "Stay behind me. I know it goes against conventional etiquette, but a woman shouldn't enter a room first, in case there's a threat inside."

The moment he pushed the door open, she grinned. "Brace yourself."

"For what?" The first dog propped its paws up on his leg and barked while the second one danced around his feet. "Hey, buddy. Get down."

"My home alarm system." When her blind miniature poodle didn't recognize Buck's smell, he dropped to his feet and barked again. "Over here, boys." She called both senior poodles to her. "It's Mama." Both dogs immediately shuffled over to Chelsea to trade sniffs and licks for a thorough petting around the ears and chest. Meanwhile, her three-legged orange tabby jumped down from the windowsill to meow loudly and plop down beside his empty food bowl. "Everybody, this is Buck. He's on our team, so be cool."

Buck might have rolled his eyes at the way she

talked to her pets as if they were tiny humans, but he didn't seem put off by being vetted by her menagerie. "One. Two. Three." He spotted the black-and-white tuxedo cat climbing out from under the day bed Chelsea kept on the back porch, then sauntering away into the kitchen, seeming bored with the whole homecoming hullabaloo. "Four." Buck glanced over his shoulder at her. "Any more I should be on the lookout for while I sweep the house?"

"They're it for now," she assured him.

Although he arched a skeptical eyebrow at the *for now* she'd added, he shut the door, threw the dead bolt and pulled her into step beside him.

Once he was certain her back room that had once been a screened-in porch was cleared, he ushered Chelsea into the kitchen and told her to wait until he checked the rest of the house. The miniature poodles trailed right after him—Raphael, with his graying black muzzle, barking at nothing in particular, and silvery Donatello with his snout practically glued to Raphael's shoulder. Looking smaller than usual next to Buck's bulk, they seemed immediately drawn to having another man on the premises and disappeared into the main part of the house with him, pleased to be running a security patrol around the house with their visitor. The dogs were panting happily by the time Buck rejoined her in the kitchen. "Everything is locked. Nothing looks tampered with."

"Thanks for checking." She picked Donatello up to drop a kiss on top of his head before returning him to his longtime partner. "These guys are great noise-makers, but I don't know if they'll scare anybody off. Donatello is blind, but his ears and nose work fine.

Raphael isn't quite as sharp, but he is Donatello's self-appointed caretaker. They've been inseparable since I adopted them."

"Donatello and Raphael? You named them after the *Teenage Mutant Ninja Turtles* characters?"

Chelsea stripped off her backpack and coat, set the first on one of the antique oak chairs at her kitchen table and carried the second into the nearby bathroom to hang over the shower curtain rod. She spared a glance in the mirror at her mangled, bloodstained sweater. Although they'd probably end up in the trash, she knew she was damn lucky there were no bullet holes in any of her clothes—or Buck's. She returned to the kitchen without changing, needing the reassurance of seeing Buck in her home more than she needed clean clothes. "There were two more—Leonardo and Michelangelo. I nursed them around the clock, but they were too sick and didn't survive. They came from a hoarding situation."

Buck reached down to scratch Raphael around the ears, and the dog immediately pushed his head into Buck's big hand to deepen the petting. "Bobby used to love the Turtles. He dressed up as the orange guy one Halloween." When the three-legged tabby brushed against his leg, he petted him, too. "Let me guess. The cats are rescues, too."

"That one's Peanut Butter because of his coloring. Despite being fixed and only having three legs, he thinks he's the stud of the house. The black-and-white one is Jelly. Mostly, she keeps to herself. She'll turn on you if she decides she doesn't like you."

"Good to know." Buck was a protective man, spoke his mind, and seemed right at home wielding a gun and chasing after bad guys. But he'd surprised her more than once tonight. He might well be the world's best hugger. He didn't ignore or dismiss her unique pets as some people did. Instead, he asked about them, petted them, and didn't seem like he was in a hurry to leave. Could any man be more perfect? Buck straightened, catching her staring at him. She quickly circled around the kitchen to pick up the animals' water bowls and carry them to the sink. "Why does it not surprise me that you rescue animals," he said.

Lexi was right—she needed to figure out what her feelings were for Buck before she tried to understand his behavior toward her. But she knew that she was attracted to the older man. Very attracted. "They need me. The house is small. But since it's only me here, there's plenty of room." She pointed out the rear window to the gentle slope and big trees of her backyard. "With this big, fenced-in yard, it makes sense to foster dogs."

"These are all fosters?"

"I've had a few over the years. These are the ones who've stayed. Donatello has memorized the layout of the house and yard, and it didn't seem fair to put him in a new place where he'd have to learn his surroundings all over again. And I would never separate him from Raphael—he's Donny's own Seeing Eye dog. As for the cats? Peanut Butter was my first adoption, and Jelly doesn't seem to like anybody else. She was returned to the shelter twice. So, they're mine. My family. A bunch of oddballs that nobody else wants." She set the dogs' water bowls in their places, then straightened with a wry smile. "That sounds sad when I say it out loud."

"No, it doesn't. You've got a big heart. You need

projects and pets to dote on." He ran his hand over Peanut Butter's back before straightening to face her across the table. "You don't see an old fart like me as one of your rescue projects, do you?"

"What? God, no." Chelsea grabbed the back of the chair where she'd stowed her bag. "You're the one who's always rescuing *me*."

"I've got both my eyes and legs, and I only snap at people who irritate me or threaten someone I care about." He crossed to the farmhouse sink. "But I am divorced and alone. Obsessed with finding Bobby to the point I don't have much of a social life beyond a regular dinner with Rufus and his wife. Or breakfast a few times a week with a special friend from the crime lab." He leaned his hips back against the countertop and crossed his arms over his chest. "I'm not handsome and I'm not charming. My last date was…hell…over a year ago?" He shrugged. "It wasn't great."

"But you're a stud. Maybe you're not movie-star handsome, but you've got testosterone oozing out your pores. There's no mistaking you for a pretty boy. You smell like a man. Your shoulders and arms are a nice package. And that sexy voice—"

"Tell me what you really think." Buck's teasing tone was husky and deep.

"That vocal quality right there. If you could do a British accent with that timbre, you could read a grocery list and my panties would melt." She slapped her hand over her mouth, her fingertips warming with the heat creeping into her cheeks. Good grief. Had she just mentioned her panties? Why did she have to ramble on without filtering out the observations and feelings zinging through her brain?

But Buck looked amused by her admission. "You're saying I've got that starship engineer or MI-6 secret agent voice, lass?" he rattled off in a perfect Scottish brogue.

Buck could do accents? His son must have picked up some of his reputed theatrical skills from his burly dad.

She *did* feel a rush of warmth at his sexy brogue. The discovery that the man had a true sense of humor made her smile with delight. "Yeah."

His whiskey-colored gaze settled on hers. "Milk. Eggs. Coffee. Bread. A wee bit of bacon. Sugar…"

A burst of heat exploded inside her and whooshed out into her fingers and toes, propelling her across the room. The impulse was as driving as it was unfamiliar. Chelsea latched on to the collar of Buck's jacket with both hands, pulled herself up onto her toes and pressed her mouth against his. His lips parted with a startled gasp, and she sucked his firm bottom lip between both of hers. The scratch of his beard stubble abraded her softer skin, exciting her with a hundred tiny caresses. She knew a split-second hesitation as she leaned into him to recapture the taut line of his mouth. Disappointment rushed in. Followed quickly by humiliation. This was one-sided. He wasn't kissing her back.

"My bad." Her cheeks burned with embarrassment. "I thought there was flirting going on. Misread the signals." But the moment she eased her grip on his jacket and dropped to her heels, Buck's big hands came up to cup either side of her face.

"No, you didn't. Hell." With a chest-deep groan he chased her lips, chased away her disappointment, and lowered his head to cover her mouth with his own.

The man who had held himself so still a moment

earlier was suddenly surrounding her, consuming her. It felt like she'd roused a sleeping dragon. His touch was hot, demanding, as he traced the seam of her lips with his tongue and forced her to open for him. His tongue swept in to dance with hers and she whimpered at the overwhelming sensations even as she cataloged each one. His mouth was hot, his lips sure. He tasted of coffee. The leather of his jacket was soft in her fists, the chest beneath it was solid, strong. She was feverish. Excited. Unafraid. Her full-on woman was roaring to life inside her. His fingers threaded into her hair, tugging a little roughly in a way that made her think Buck was losing control. The tips of his fingers pulsed against her scalp, holding her mouth beneath his as he plundered it. This was no get-acquainted kiss. No finding out what she liked or didn't and then trying something else. This was raw. This was need. This was a man taking exactly what he wanted. This was every sensual thing she'd ever dreamed about in a kiss but hadn't known existed until Buck. Until this moment. He turned her and backed her against the sink, never breaking contact with her lips. His thighs rocked into hers and she felt the outline of his muscular body pressing into her curves, claiming her.

Chelsea had never been claimed before.

She'd experienced a few tame make-out sessions in the years since she'd learned to tolerate a man's touch again. But she'd never initiated a kiss. She'd never succumbed to this aching fire racing through her veins, ignited by such a powerful, confident touch. She'd never wanted a kiss the way she was craving this one. She'd never been hungry, no—starving—for something more.

Chelsea uncurled her fingers from his jacket so that she could move her arms that were trapped between them and slide them around his neck. She didn't want even that barrier between them. She was excited to feel his hardness notched at the juncture of her thighs. She wanted to feel his strength and heat against her entire body. She wanted in a way she'd never wanted with any other man.

But the moment she palmed the back of his neck and dragged her fingers across his short, crisp hair, he released her to grab her wrists. Muttering a harsh curse, Buck pulled her hands away and retreated a step. She felt a sudden chill circling around her, as if she was lying on that cold, wet pavement again.

By the time she realized her glasses had steamed up, he'd released her entirely and put the length of the room between them.

She pulled off her glasses and wiped them on the hem of her blouse, squinting his dark bulk into focus. "What's wrong?"

"Nothing." He cursed again, his breathing as deep and uneven as her own. "Everything."

She put her glasses back on and tried to read his glowering expression. "I don't understand. Are you all right? Did I do something wrong? I don't have a lot of experience, but—"

"If you apologize for what happened—"

"—it seemed like the right thing to do in that moment. I wanted that kiss. I thought you did, too. I'm sorry if I made you uncomfortable."

"There it is. There's the apology." Buck stalked into the sunporch, ignoring the dogs trailing after him as he headed to the door. "I'm not one of your rescue projects."

She shooed Raphael aside, and Donatello shifted course with him, as she hurried to catch Buck. "I didn't think you were—"

He whirled around on her with such force that she drew back a step. "I need you to find my son, and I need you to be safe. I don't *need* anything else from you."

"Oh. Okay." Chelsea hugged her arms around her waist. Why was he so angry? What was she missing here? "I thought we were sharing some stuff and flirting and getting closer. After everything tonight... I thought you felt that chemistry, too, but... I understand."

"I wish you did. Hell, I wish I did." After a long hesitation, he scrubbed his palm across his jaw, taking the anger from his expression and leaving something that looked like pain in his eyes. "I didn't scare you, did I? I didn't remind you of Hunt or your foster dad?"

"What?" He thought she could respond like that to a man who frightened or abused her? "No. God, no. I liked it," she confessed to a fraction of what she'd been feeling. "More than I ever thought I could." Was that what had made him withdraw so abruptly? "I've never felt like that with a man before," she confessed. "Like I couldn't get close enough to you, like I couldn't get enough. You weren't hurting me. I wasn't afraid. It was...liberating." She frowned. "You couldn't tell how much I wanted you? I must not have been doing it right."

His nostrils flared with a deep breath and then he was all business. "It's been a long night. Lock this door behind me. Get some sleep. I'll be back to drive you to the lab."

Chelsea was stunned by how quickly a man could go from protective to bossy to comforting to funny to sexy to protective and bossy again in such a short time. How was she supposed to interpret and understand such rapid-fire emotional changeups like that? "Okay."

He swiped his palm over the top of his head, leaving the short spikes in a rumpled mess. "You're too sweet for me to resist. And you weren't doing a damn thing wrong. You were sexy and responsive and for a few seconds there I felt like I was ten feet tall and ten years younger. This is on me. I'm sorry I let that kiss get out of hand. I didn't mean to take advantage of you."

"You didn't. I started it—"

"I blame fatigue and rusty hormones. Like I said, it's been a long time since I've been on a date. And this wasn't even a date."

"I get it," she snapped. Way to kill the buzz of arousal she'd been feeling. She thought they'd shared one hell of a kiss. He thought it had been a mistake.

"Chelsea, I'm thirteen years older than you. A grown man ought to know better than to think with anything other than his brain. I'm sorry. That kiss shouldn't have happened."

Funny. She didn't like hearing him apologize any more than he detested it with her. Her tone sharpened with an unfamiliar bite. "I was just a woman kissing a man. Not an older man. Not a scary man. Just a man I wanted to kiss. It won't happen again."

"I'm not blaming you. It's not like you were doing it all by yourself." He scrubbed his face again, in a rough attempt to regain control of his reaction to her romantic overture. "Damn it, Chels, I'm not handling this right."

That made two of them. "You and I are both beyond tired. So, let's stop talking about it." She went to the door to hold it open for him. "Good night, Buck. Thank you again for saving me from all those bullets tonight."

He hesitated at the door, looking down at the top of her head while she stared at the butterfly bandage over the cut on his cheek. She could still feel his heat and smell the piney soap on his skin. Damn, she could still taste him in her mouth. They'd crossed a line tonight she wasn't sure how to come back from.

"If you get any more threats, call me. Or text." His voice was a deep-pitched whisper that skittered across her eardrums. "If you still trust me enough to do that."

When she didn't immediately answer, he slipped a blunt finger under her chin to tilt her gaze up to his. He was waiting for some acknowledgement of his directive.

Chelsea pulled her chin from his touch but maintained eye contact. "I trust you, Buck."

Buck held her gaze until she had to look away. Then he was on his way out the door. "Good night."

He waited for her to lock the knob and the dead bolt before he stepped off the porch and climbed into his truck. Chelsea softly banged her forehead against the doorframe, feeling buffeted by waves of confusion, humiliation and pain.

What the hell had she been thinking? Buck was her friend. She needed a friend like him in her life, and she had probably done irreparable damage to that relationship. Why hadn't she thought through that sudden, blazing need to kiss the stuffing out of him?

Chelsea put the dogs out for a quick run around the yard. It felt as if there were eyes on her from somewhere in the darkness—like she was being watched, hunted.

She hurried back into the house to wait for them to do their business. Hugging her arms around herself, she realized she didn't feel any safer with a locked door between her and the threat her overactive imagination had conjured.

The only place she'd felt truly safe tonight—over the past few months—maybe in her entire life—was with Buck. And she might just have chased away her sanctuary with one impulsive, misguided, but amazing, kiss.

Chapter Seven

Chelsea felt the cool nose of a poodle snuffling around her ankle, followed by the imprint of two small paws above her knee, as she stood at the stove to brew a cup of green tea to help her wired brain fall asleep. She looked down and smiled at wise old Donatello with his blank eyes. He might not be able to see, but he always seemed to know when something was amiss in his world. "Hey, baby." She reached down to scoop the dog into her arms and rub her nose into the soft curls of his graying hair. "I didn't mean to wake you boys up. I can't stop thinking about Buck."

Chelsea scratched her fingers around the dog's ears, finding comfort in the knowledge that someone around here wanted her touch. She should have recognized Buck's initial shock at an invasion of his personal space. She should have retreated before he turned the tables on her and kissed her back and filled her head with ideas about desire and a pent-up need to get closer. He'd petted her dogs and Peanut Butter. He was the kind of man she'd always wanted in her life. Safe. But not in the boring sense.

Safe and sexy. Safe and interesting. Safe enough

to be herself with. Safe and…damn, that man was a great kisser.

She could still feel his hands on her face and in her hair, still taste the stamp of his lips claiming her mouth, the raspy stroke of his tongue dancing with hers. The only thing she regretted about Buck's kiss was that it had ended so abruptly.

No, what she regretted was that she'd changed the status of their relationship and made things weird between them. Instead of teasing banter and bossy directives, holding hands and subtle touches, now she had hard looks and terse words and a dutiful promise to still protect her despite his adamant misgivings about letting things go too far with her. She doubted she'd even be getting one of those sweetly frustrating forehead kisses now.

She'd confirmed what she'd told Lexi earlier. Buck thought of her as an asset—not a woman he could be interested in.

She'd do well to remember that.

Chelsea set Donatello down, and Raphael eagerly joined him to get his share of petting, too. After a few minutes of spoiling her pets and improving her mood—or at least finding the will to push the lingering thoughts about that kiss to the back of her mind—Chelsea gave them each a treat, picked up her tea and headed back to bed.

After spending a few minutes straightening the covers where she'd been tossing and turning earlier, Chelsea admitted to herself that she probably wasn't going to fall asleep until she could turn off her brain. And that wasn't going to happen until she could find an answer to at least one thing tonight. So, she pulled out her laptop and carried it into the spare bedroom she'd converted into her own mini computer lab, complete with multiple screens and keyboards, a web of surge protectors and power cords. She paid her cable company for more gigawatts of power than the average home computer system, treating her setup like the business it was. She turned on the laptop, then plugged it in beside her desktop computer to let the battery recharge. She wanted to do an in-depth search to see if she could find the video clips from Sin City that had vanished from her screen. Not that she was any more rested and clearheaded now than she'd been at the bar, but her amped-up connections here could run scans and even retrieve information she might have accidentally launched into cyberspace. First, she needed to find those images. Then, she'd run a resolution software program to see if she could pull up usable intel like a motorcycle tag number off the screenshots.

Forget Buck and unrequited crushes. It made a sad sort of sense in her screwed-up life to discover that the one man she wanted didn't want her. Or didn't *want* to want her. She should probably be grateful to prove that she had healed enough from the abuse and assault to desire a man again. Maybe there was something to what Buck was saying—maybe she was attracted to him because he was safe. But nothing about that kiss had felt safe. It had felt wild, sensual, grown-up. Normal.

Was it too much to ask for a relationship like the one Lexi and Aiden enjoyed? A soul-deep connection. Some sexy times. A few laughs. Unflinching support. Absolute trust.

Apparently, she wasn't a good candidate for *normal*.

Technology was her truest companion. Her pets didn't care if she was socially awkward. She didn't doubt her friendship with Buck.

But she was beginning to doubt she could ever be anything more than the crime lab's resident computer savant, or the special needs foster parent the local animal shelter had on speed dial.

While her system was booting up, she wound her hair into a loose bun on the top of her head. The dogs settled onto their rug with their chewy treats, and Peanut Butter curled up on the bed behind her desk. Jelly was scratching in the litter box on the sunporch, and Chelsea suspected she wouldn't see the tuxedo cat until time for breakfast.

Once the icons on her screen appeared, Chelsea pulled up the internet and clicked on her email.

She opened the first message and gasped.

"What the hell…?"

Lose something?

Attached to the message were the two pictures she'd misplaced. Both had been altered. The first had been drawn on with a paint tool, the childlike doodles of curly hair and a clown costume effectively obscuring the man at her car. In the second, the license plate and gun had been blurred to the point that the photo was almost entirely black except for the word *Bang* written across it in dripping red letters.

This was no accidental email glitch. And she didn't recognize the sender. Not that she believed *Trouble@ haha.com* meant anything good.

Green tea wasn't enough to calm her anymore. Fear-ing what she'd find when she logged back into Vinnie's security feed to grab the original images, she pushed her mug aside to pull up tonight's video log. Chelsea reminded herself to breathe. In. Out. Don't. Panic.

She didn't even have to double-check the time stamp when she pulled up the grainy video feed. She knew this was the recording she needed. But there was nothing there. No man. No car. No gun. Everything had been erased. Not that they'd been particularly helpful images to begin with, but at least she'd had something to go on to try to figure out the shooter's identity. Now she had nothing.

She let the staticky feed play for another two minutes until she heard the metallic ping of another incoming message. Closing down the blank security footage from the bar, she clicked on the new email.

She recoiled from her keyboard.

Stay in your own corner of the web, bitch.

You've been warned. If I find you in my business again, I'll be the Trouble you don't want to mess with.

The unsigned message was followed by row after row of laughing-face emoticons that she didn't find funny at all filling her screen.

How had this guy gotten her private email address? How had he gotten into her laptop? She had layers upon layers of security on her equipment. *She* was the hacker. No one got through her firewalls and broke her code.

But there it was, laughing at her. More sophisticated than the handwritten message on her car tonight.

More frightening because a computer was the one place where she was queen. Her specialized knowledge and technical expertise were her domain. There were no people to misread or mistrust online. No mistakes. No one could hurt her in cyberspace.

Until tonight. Not until *Trouble* busted into her world and started laughing at her.

He'd pulled off some pretty sophisticated computer work to steal those pictures. Breaking into Vinnie's security system to alter the feed meant this *Trouble* either had the password, or he was a talented hacker.

Losing those pictures hadn't been a fluke. She hadn't made a mistake. *Trouble* had cloned her system and gotten access to everything on her laptop.

Shivering, Chelsea slowly rolled her chair away from the desk, as if distance could erase the feeling of violation creeping through her.

What had she done to make somebody angry like this?

Chelsea pulled the old turquoise hoodie off the back of her chair and shrugged into it. But she still couldn't stop shaking.

She didn't need warmer clothes. She needed Buck.

She unplugged her phone from its charger. She wanted to hear his voice. She glanced at the time. It was nearly four in the morning. Maybe he'd already gone to bed and wouldn't answer. But it wouldn't hurt to at least text him.

Her thumbs flew over the screen.

U awake?

Just showered and heading to bed. What are you doing up?

Now that he'd answered, what was she supposed to tell him? *I got freaked out by a couple of emails? I need you to drive back across town and make me feel safe? Could you forget about that kiss and give me another one of those bear hugs? And, seriously, are you telling me you're naked?*

Why couldn't she think?

She scooted back to her laptop, wondering if snapping a picture of the threat and sending it to him would explain everything she didn't know how to say.

His message came through first.

Chels? You're not apologizing for that kiss again, are you? Maybe it was inevitable that it finally happened. There's a weird chemistry between us.

Weird. That's what every woman wanted to hear after an earthshaking kiss.

I'm not sorry. I don't care about the 13 years. It didn't feel weird to me. It felt right. Until you thought it didn't. Then I was embarrassed.

Don't be. I was far from an unwilling participant. For the record, I've never lost control like that with a woman before. You surprised me. My reaction surprised me. But as much as I wanted that kiss, I'm not sure the timing is right. Not sure I'm the right man for you. Thought I'd better leave before anything else happened we might regret.

I don't regret anything. But I hate fighting with you. Are we still friends?

She didn't really want an answer to that, did she? She'd already been enough of an imposition. He'd said a lot of things that she needed to clarify in her head. They'd touched each other a lot tonight—held hands, hugged, kissed. And not being the right man for her? Had she ever imagined anyone else embracing her like that? Had she ever wanted a man the way she wanted Buck?

When he didn't immediately answer that last text, she looked at the laptop. The one thing she was good at. Reading people? Understanding emotions and sexual attraction? Not so much. But computers? She didn't need any old-school alpha male to help with that. *Trouble* might have bested her tonight, but she hadn't realized she was under attack.

Why was she under attack? What corner of the web had she violated?

Her phone beeped with Buck's reply.

Absolutely. It wasn't a fight, sweetheart. We were laying down some ground rules we should have talked about sooner.

Sweetheart. Ground rules. Which one was she supposed to believe? The endearment that indicated she meant something to him? Or the phrase that sounded like he wanted to keep his distance from her? And would knowing the right answer make a difference in Buck coming to her rescue again? No. She didn't need to be rescued from an email. Bullets could hurt her, but an email couldn't.

She typed in her response.

Thanks for everything tonight. I wasn't as scared as I would have been without you.

I've got no problem protecting you.

Just a problem with kissing her and turning their friendship into something more.

She shouldn't have started this conversation. She was tired of being afraid and alone. But she wouldn't force herself on Buck again. She pushed the raw emotions from her thoughts.

What time will you pick me up for work?

7 too early? We could grab breakfast on the way to the lab.

Meet for breakfast. Like they always did. As friends. She shouldn't feel so disappointed.

Fine.

Are you okay? Why aren't you sleeping?

The devil in her prompted her to type, If I said I needed you, what would you do?

I'd come running.

The feeling of being cherished, of being important enough to someone that they'd drop everything and come to her aid, rushed through her—soothed her fear, strengthened her. But it was followed just as quickly by a figurative slap on the face, the mental reminder that Chelsea was alone in the world, that she couldn't sustain a relationship, that she wasn't the kind of woman that a man like Buck wanted.

OK.

Do you need me?

She glanced over at the threat on her screen. She typed Yes, then deleted it. She wasn't going to cause Buck any more trouble. Not tonight. He deserved to get at least a couple hours of sleep.

I like talking to you. Even if it's a text conversation like this. I was worried I might have ruined that.

You mean something to me. I don't want to lose that connection, either.

He meant a lot to her, too. Why couldn't she say how much she needed him right now? Would he really reject her? She could feel her breathing even out, just by chatting with him. The furnace had come on and the shivering had stopped. Buck's texts had centered her, given her a chance to focus. She shouldn't ask for anything more.

What aren't you telling me?

She stared at his message, wanting to answer. Wanting to tell him how scared she was that *Trouble* had entered her cyber world and threatened her. But she was equally afraid Buck would never see her as anything more than that asset he felt honor-bound to protect.

Chels?????

See you at 7. Good night.

Chelsea shut off her phone and plugged it back into its charger. She didn't need any brawny protector to hold her hand. This was where she shone.

Was Dennis Hunt savvy enough to hack his way into her private account? She wouldn't have thought so. If he was this good, the crime lab wouldn't have hired her. Gordy Bismarck probably didn't even own a computer, much less have the expertise to track down a private email address. But he did have a lot of criminal friends. One of them might be a hacker.

She couldn't think of any work-related investigations that would warrant sending her a threat like this. She was a behind-the-scenes support technician. And she certainly wasn't a detective who could make an arrest.

But she knew enough detectives and retired cops to think like one.

Why was *Trouble* capitalized in the middle of the message? Why choose it for the email address? It sounded like a handle, the kind of nickname a black hat hacker would use to showcase his mastery of the online world while hiding his identity. Although she considered herself a white hat—a good guy—hacker, she had a handle herself that she used online for some of the more dubious activities she'd engaged in before finding her calling doing legitimate work for the crime lab.

Yes, she'd done some dark web searches in her quest to find a lead on Bobby Buckner. But she'd been careful to cover her trail each time. Besides, she hadn't found anything useful. The DNA lead she'd shared with Buck tonight had come through a legitimate source, matching a genealogy profile to a KCPD cold case report. The other DNA matches had popped up the same way—someone had gotten their DNA analyzed, and the results had been uploaded onto various databases where they hadn't existed before. Her search bots had pinged on them the moment they'd become available.

Those uploads were traceable.

Emails were traceable.

She was certain this *Trouble* would have covered his tracks. But she was a pro at uncovering digital trails.

Chelsea set her mug down beside the keyboard, finally feeling warm again. She could do this. She rolled her neck to ease the weary kinks of going nearly twenty-four hours without sleep. Then she went to work.

Some bully had hacked her email and threatened her.

She couldn't do anything about embarrassing herself by wanting a man who didn't feel the same way about her. Maybe that was a skill she would never learn.

But when it came to computers, *Trouble* didn't know who he was messing with.

Chapter Eight

There wasn't enough coffee in the world to make up for all the sleep Buck had been deprived of lately. He'd hoped that with Vinnie closing the bar for a couple of nights after the shooting Chelsea would stay home. But she was as determined as she was unpredictable, and she'd insisted that Vinnie needed her whether Sin City was open for business or not.

Playing bodyguard to Chelsea meant Buck went where she did. And since he wasn't one to sit around and twiddle his thumbs, he'd ended up chasing off some stragglers from the motorcycle club who refused to accept that the bar was closed while she was inside helping Vinnie clean up the place and mentally regroup after the shooting. He'd even helped Martin the drunk, who seemed to have no other residence than the corner barstool, sober up and get safely to the nearby Yankee Hill Shelter for the night. Buck had installed a new set of security cameras and traded stories with Vinnie about a few funny and frightening adventures at Sin City over the years. Fortunately, there hadn't been another shooting incident, or any other obvious threats.

But there hadn't been any more sweet, funny or cryptic late-night conversations with Chelsea, either.

No lectures about his addiction to caffeine. No disjointed essay about her latest research, or tangential question about something personal. Not even a lousy emoticon in a text.

Buck felt like he'd lost something important.

And it was his own damn fault.

He never should have kissed her. He never should have surrendered to his baser desires like that. And he damn sure shouldn't be wanting to kiss her again. And yet, every lonesome, aching cell in his body did. He wanted her in his shower. In his bed. He wanted her snugged in his arms when he woke up in the morning. He wanted to talk in funny accents and see her eyes light up with laughter. He wanted all of that. All of her.

And now he felt as though he didn't have anything beyond the professional working relationship they'd started with months ago.

Buck had no clue how to recapture the easy odd-couple friendship they'd shared. At the very least, he intended to keep her safe, as he'd promised. But his brain, his body and his heart wanted a lot more than *the very least* with Chelsea. Not the smartest impulse for a man his age. But he wanted it all the same.

Her last meaningful conversation was still tattooed on his brain.

If I said I needed you, what would you do?

I'd come running.

He should have asked what she'd do if he confessed to how badly he needed her. Her smiles. Her quirky insights. Her trust. Her caring.

Now he'd been reduced to bodyguard and chauffeur status. And not even the fun kind where he was Malcolm MacDougal MacPherson and she grinned and giggled at his silly Scottish accent.

Buck drank another swallow from his travel mug as he leaned against the doorframe of the Kansas City Crime Lab's conference room, letting the burn running down his gullet irritate his senses into staying sharp. The crime lab's director, Mac Taylor, had invited Buck to join the Friday morning briefing as an observer, and to answer any questions he could to help them direct their investigation into Wednesday night's shooting at the bar. He was used to meetings like this— he'd answered shift roll calls for twenty years as a cop. Concerns to be on the lookout for. Prioritization of casework. Breaks on investigations to follow up on. Pinpointing issues where extra help might be needed. Team morale.

Scanning the criminalists and support staff seated around the table, Buck felt Mac had his work cut out for him on that last one. One of their own had been attacked, and they'd been working almost around the clock to find answers as to who and why. Faces were grim and tired. Or maybe that was the filter Buck was viewing them through, from his own perspective this morning.

Even though he wasn't officially a part of the crime lab team, Buck had worked with several of the criminalists, both during his twenty years with the department and more recently with his security firm subcontracting some of their routine work. Early in both their public service careers, he'd been a uniformed officer on patrol when Mac Taylor had been caught in an explosion that had scarred his face and cost him the sight in one eye. The Taylor name was synonymous with solid, honorable police work in Kansas City, and over the years, he'd worked a few cases with Mac and his detective brothers, Josh and Cole, and his cousin Mitch, who was now serving as chief of police.

He recognized others in the room, too. Grayson Malone, the Marine Corps combat veteran and blood analysis expert, sat in his wheelchair at the opposite end of the table from Mac. Standing behind him, leaning against the corner cupboard, was Jackson Dobbs. One of the biggest dudes Buck had ever met who wasn't playing professional football, Dobbs was hard to get to know because he seemed to keep to himself unless he was working an investigation. But his knowledge of weaponry was vast, and Buck had appreciated his focus on processing Chelsea's car and getting some answers to work with. Next to Malone at the table was Shane Duvall. Buck didn't think the man was really a professor, but his glasses and beard gave him that nerdy intellectual vibe. Buck knew the B shift supervisor, Lexi Callahan, with her chin-length golden brown hair, was Chelsea's best friend. Behind her stood her fiancée, Aiden Murphy, a K-9 cop who provided security when the CSIs were called to process a crime scene in a potentially dangerous location. He could hear the panting of Aiden's partner, a Belgian Malinois named Blue, from somewhere near Aiden's feet, where the athletic dog and unofficial crime lab mascot was resting. The Black woman next to Lexi, Khari Thomas, had recently returned from maternity leave, and had the pretty glow and drooping eyes of a new mother that his Mary had had those first few months after Bobby was born. Zoe Stockman, with long dark hair pulled up in a messy bun on top of her head, was the new kid on the team, eagerly hanging on to Mac's every word and looking a little overwhelmed, as usual.

Then there was Chelsea herself.

Sweet, one-of-a-kind Chelsea who'd suffered so much and still wore her heart on her sleeve. She focused on others and was giving to the point she risked her own health and welfare. She gave to her special needs pets. Her friends. Vinnie. Buck himself.

She sat at the end of the table, next to Mac. Her elbow was on the table beside her ubiquitous laptop, her chin resting in her hand. This morning, her long, wavy hair was pulled back into a ponytail, and she wore tortoiseshell-framed glasses that reminded him of pictures from a 1950s yearbook. If he wasn't mistaken, the eyes behind those lenses were closed. But he knew she wasn't sleeping because she kept stroking the edge of her laptop with her free hand, as if unwilling to break contact with the technology she lived and breathed.

He knew how Chelsea's brain chugged away, going ninety miles a minute, thinking in a dozen different directions, maybe so she didn't have to concentrate on the problems of the present or a bad memory for too long. She followed her instincts more than her common sense, and he'd seen firsthand how those impulses could get her into trouble. But other than that day when she'd confessed all the crap Dennis Hunt had been putting her through, she greeted him every morning he'd seen her with a smile. It burned a hole in his gut to think that this time *he* was the one who'd stolen that smile from her.

His gut was telling him something was wrong. But since she wasn't talking and he wasn't telepathic, he had no idea what that could be. Had she received another threat? If she had but wasn't telling him because of the way he'd broken things between them, then he needed to make it right. Chelsea being afraid or suffering alone was not an option he could live with.

He heard a soft ding from her computer, and her eyes popped open. She glanced at the screen and frowned. She clicked the mouse and started to type before she remembered she was in the middle of a meeting and glanced up at Mac to apologize for the interruption. "Sorry."

"Not a problem," Mac assured her. "It's not the first time one of my staff has worked through a meeting. Anything we need to know about?"

Her gaze darted to Buck's then back to her screen. "I got an ID on that John Doe murder victim through my facial recognition trace." Mac cleared his throat, waiting for the rest of the information she was silently reading. "Oh, um, Yuri Dubrovnik. He's a Lukinburg national. He flew into KCI the day before his body was found…" She looked up at Mac. "Their drug agency has a BOLO out on him."

Buck pushed away from the doorframe. "My son wouldn't have anything to do with drug smuggling or a fugitive from the law."

"Easy, Buck," Mac warned. "We're a long way from accusing anyone of murder yet. Dubrovnik could be one of their agents. I'll put a call in to the embassy. Aleks Petrovic has worked with KCPD before. Hopefully, he can find us some answers."

Buck's gaze drifted down to the compassion shining

in Chelsea's eyes. But she quickly blinked and looked back to her screen. "That's not the only information that's popped up in the last forty-eight hours."

"More DNA matches?" Mac asked.

She nodded.

"Keep tracking them. We're a good team. But I'm not buying that we're suddenly going to clear two dozen cases in a matter of days because DNA matches to previously unknown subjects are falling into our laps."

"Someone has to be manipulating this data," Chelsea murmured. She clicked and scrolled with her mouse. "No way."

Mac noticed her distracted tone, too. "Something else?"

When she didn't answer, Buck took half a step into the crowded room. Mac wasn't the only one who noticed Chelsea's preoccupation with her laptop. "Chels?"

Her skin blanched beneath that dusting of freckles. He wished he could understand what was going on behind those beautiful eyes. Did she have bad news about Bobby? Good news? Any news? Or was she overwhelmed by the sudden influx of data her research had triggered? Was there something else he was missing here? He began to think he was reading fear rather than fatigue there, but Chelsea resumed typing. "It's nothing." She waved at Mac to continue as if she was the one running this meeting. "Nothing more to report, I mean. I'm cataloging everything. I need time to process it."

Hating the look that shuttered her expression and feeling guilty for being the boor who had changed the openness between them, Buck countered by taking another drink of coffee, grimacing at the acidic burn.

He needed a new habit. Caffeine, guilt and stress were really doing a number on his insides. About the only thing that gave him any relief was...Chelsea. Those big, green-gold eyes. That beautiful smile. Conversation that kept him on his toes. A passionate kiss. All those things that were uniquely her—they pulled him out of the dark place and made him feel better. Happy. Hopeful.

All these months he thought he was the big, bad-ass protector. That Chelsea needed him to have her back and defend her from the dangers of the world while she got lost in her work and technology or followed her heart without thinking it through.

But Chelsea was a survivor. She'd faced hell more than once in her life, and she'd come through it without being jaded. She'd been hurt, but she could still smile, still care. In terms of spirit and courage, she was the strongest person he'd ever known.

He was the one who needed *her*.

Still coming to terms with that revelation, Buck tuned out the rest of the meeting until he heard Mac's final agenda item. The director reached over to squeeze Chelsea's shoulder, interrupting her typing. "I don't like that someone's taking potshots at one of us. Thanks to Buck, Chelsea's okay." Buck didn't need the thanks from the men and women around the room. He wanted to know what was making Mac look like a man with bad news. "Legal tells me that Dennis Hunt's lawyer is looking to make a plea deal for restitution and time served. He'll probably lose his accreditation. But that's a slap on the wrist in the grand scheme of things."

"What?" Lexi was the first one to chime in. "He's not in jail *now*." She reached across the table to clasp

Chelsea's hand, whose eyes were wide-open now. "No. Not good enough. He hurt us, Mac. He strangled me. And Chels…" Her voice trailed away, not wanting to publicly share the assault Chelsea had gone through.

Buck's blood steamed at the pale cast to Chelsea's skin. He would have stormed into the room and told Mac in no uncertain terms what Legal could do with Hunt's deal, when Mac raised his hands to placate the group. "Do not shoot the messenger. My point is this," he continued in that coolly logical voice of his. "I'm not allowing Hunt to get away with the crimes he committed here. But we all know what a narcissistic egomaniac he is. He's going to try to get out of this one way or another." His gaze circled the room. "Can we tie him to the shooting?"

Jackson responded first. "Not yet. The rounds came from a Glock 9 mil. Hunt doesn't own a gun."

"Doesn't mean he can't steal one or hire someone to do his dirty work," Aiden grumbled. "I should have let Blue take a chunk out of him when I arrested his ass."

Mac let his people grumble their frustration but kept the meeting moving forward. "What about the trace you found on that slug?"

"Lip balm," Shane answered.

Mac turned to Khari for elaboration. "Could you pull any DNA?"

The woman nodded, but she was frowning. "Male donor. But even with all the new IDs Chelsea's getting, there's no match in our system."

Lexi grumbled something under her breath before shaking her head in frustration. "Dennis is in the system. I took that swab myself. He'd show up as a match. We can't prove he shot at Chelsea."

Buck watched the lump travel down Chelsea's throat as she swallowed hard. "What did I do wrong?"

"Nothing," Lexi insisted, squeezing Chelsea's hand again. "None of this is your fault. You're a truth finder. Dennis and all those cockroaches who hide in the shadows can't stand the truth being brought to light. You're brave and smart, and they can't handle you revealing what they want to keep hidden."

Lexi calmed as Aiden's hands came up to massage her shoulders, and Buck glimpsed Blue's black nose and snout nuzzling Chelsea's lap, offering his support. The dog was giving the comfort Buck wanted to provide. Buck acknowledged the stab of jealousy for a dog and quickly buried it. It was for the best to let her turn to the animals she loved so well. Until he sorted his feelings out about her, it was probably a smarter move to not get any more involved with Chelsea than he already was.

Buck retreated another step, surrendering the place he wanted to be to the dog as Mac continued. "Get with the detectives on the case and let's confirm Hunt's alibi for the shooting. If it checks out, I want a court order to run his finances. I want to know if he paid someone to scare Chelsea. I don't want to shortchange our other cases, but this is priority one. Find me a lead. Let's prove witness intimidation against Hunt or find out who else has it in for her and get this perp behind bars. Until then—" Mac's good eye was piercing as he looked across the room to meet Buck's gaze "—we keep our computer expert safe."

Buck's chest swelled with a resolute breath, and he exchanged a sharp nod with Mac. Even if he'd given the protection assignment to Aiden and Blue, or called in another cop to shadow Chelsea, Buck intended to be on her protection detail.

Buck drifted back into the hallway as Mac dismissed the meeting and the room emptied out. Since he was going to be here at the lab complex shadowing Chelsea for the foreseeable future, Buck turned and headed to the memorial lounge to refill his mug with some fresh java.

He stopped at the soft tug on the sleeve of his suit jacket and looked down into Chelsea's frowning face. "You drink too much of that stuff. You already had three cups at breakfast." Since her arms were full of her laptop, she nodded toward the travel mug. "It's probably eating away your insides and wreaking havoc with your heart rate and blood pressure."

There was the reprimand he'd missed this morning. His lips softened their grim line as something like relief eased the tension gripping him.

"You don't have to take care of me, Chels." Especially when she was the one who needed someone watching over her. "I'm a grown man."

"You're a grown man who's going to get an ulcer," she chided. "It'll make you grumpier than you already are. If you won't look after yourself, then someone else needs to."

He wanted to smile at her rebuke. He definitely needed someone like her in his life. But that wasn't what their relationship was supposed to be about. "I'm not a rescue project of yours," he warned, even as his heart warmed to the familiar debate. "Let it go."

"Just trying to be a friend," she explained, revealing an unfamiliar snap to her voice. "You said that's what you wanted from me. Speaking of…" She adjusted her glasses on the bridge of her nose, drawing his attention to the shadows beneath her eyes. Damn, she looked like a brainy coed who'd pulled an all-nighter cramming for a final test—a cute, *sexy* coed, his body announced. But Buck forced himself to listen to the *young* connotation of the coed observation his brain was making, and not what the interest in every other cell of his body was telling him. "Actually, I'm changing the subject completely—could I talk to you later?" She patted the edge of her laptop. "There's a thing I need to show you."

"What thing?"

"Well, a couple of things." Any chill he heard in her tone a moment ago had vanished. "I need to set up a program for Grayson before I can take a break. He's the one who's gotten stuck following up all these DNA matches to determine which ones are legit. I can at least help him categorize the sources of the samples. Do you have time to wait?"

Had she missed that whole silent interchange between him and her boss? "I've cleared my schedule with my office manager for the next few days. I'm not going anywhere."

She glanced up and down the hallway as her crowd of coworkers thinned, then leaned in and whispered, "I found something after you left the other night that I've been looking into. And just now, I got another message."

"A message?"

He hated when she stopped making eye contact with him. Her gaze landed on the lapel of his tweedy jacket, darted back and forth, then settled onto a particularly interesting nub of wool again. Then she simply shook her head.

Buck tucked a finger beneath her chin and tilted her face up to his. Even with the lenses of her glasses making her eyes appear smaller, he could read the fear stamped there. "What's happened?"

"Sorry to interrupt." Gray Malone swung his wheelchair up beside them, the stumps of his amputated legs forming a lap to hold file folders, his computer tablet and his phone. "Chelsea? We're ready for your report on that cascade of DNA matches you've been working." He skimmed his hand over dark blond hair that was still cut high and tight in military style. "I don't want to turn anything over to the Cold Case Squad until we can confirm the source."

"I'll be right there to show you how to run the program. The statistics of that many hits to unsolved cases is skewed if you ask me, but they might be worth following up on. It's how I found those links to Bobby Buckner."

"Those?" Buck pressed. She'd found out something else about his son? "More than one?"

She glanced up at Buck. "Will you wait?"

As anxious and concerned as he was about whatever she wanted to tell him, Buck knew she had to work. *He* was the extracurricular activity here. "Of course."

Gray lifted his chin to Buck. "Don't worry. I'll have eyes on her until she gets back to you."

The veteran might be limited to a wheelchair or prostheses now, but Grayson Malone was still in fighting shape—broad-shouldered, muscular and fit. If he said Chelsea would be safe under his watch, Buck believed him. He nodded his appreciation. "I'll be in the lounge."

"Thank you." Chelsea fell into step beside Gray's chair, passing the uniformed officer coming around the corner. The man who had been Buck's former partner on the force smiled down at her, even as she gave him a warning. "Sergeant? Don't let Buck refill that mug."

Rufus King chuckled and offered Chelsea a salute. "Yes, ma'am." He watched her and Gray disappear around the corner before propping his hands at the top of his holster and utility belt and joining Buck. "You got a new wife I don't know about?"

"Let it go," Buck warned. "She likes to take care of people."

"You could use a little taking care of," Rufus observed, chucking a fist at Buck's stubbled chin. He'd skipped shaving this morning in favor of an extra ten minutes of sleep, which turned out to be fitful and useless in recharging his batteries. "She looks like death warmed over. Which is only half as bad as you look."

"Gee, thanks."

"Walk with me, partner." Rufus clapped Buck on the shoulder and led him past the floor-to-ceiling windows to the end of the hallway. "Rumor has it you've been in a mood. I heard you had to be a cop again at Sin City."

"You mean getting shot at?" Buck shrugged it off, falling back on the wry, dark humor he and the cops he knew often used to deal with the emotional highs and lows of the job. "Felt like old times."

Rufus grinned. "What else happened besides the shooting?" Rufus knew better than to stop Buck from refilling his coffee mug, but by the time he had replaced the lid and pulled out a stool at one of the high-topped tables across from his friend, Buck found he had little desire to keep drinking the fake fuel. Plus, if it made Chelsea worry, he could suck it up and go without. She had enough on her plate already without adding him to her list of concerns. "This is me. I can read you like a book, my friend. There's tension between you and Chelsea. You have an argument?"

Buck rolled the travel mug between his hands before he pushed it aside and leaned back in his seat. There was no sense lying to his friend. Diving into work yesterday hadn't given Buck any answers. Maybe talking this thing through would help him get his head back where it needed to be, instead of reliving that kiss. Every time he thought he could dismiss the incident, the memory of her grasping hands clinging to him, her soft, sexy hair tangled in his fingers, her sweet, eager lips dueling with his own surged to the forefront, reminding him how turned on he'd been. It was as if he'd finally found the thing he didn't know he'd been searching for. With Chelsea in his arms, everything had fallen into place. He'd been alive. For those few brief minutes, saying goofy things and making her smile, seeing her throw herself at him and initiate that kiss—he'd been happy. For a few blessed minutes he hadn't felt raw with grief and worry.

"I kissed her," Buck confessed. "Well, she kissed me, and I didn't protest."

"Didn't protest?" Rufus snorted a skeptical sound trough his nose. "You mean that skinny thing pinned you down and forced herself on you?"

Skinny? That wasn't the impression he'd gotten of that perfect bottom and those perky, responsive breasts. "You're giving me grief and then you want me to confide in you? All right. One, that woman has curves you can't begin to know about beneath those colorful clothes she wears, and two… I might have taken over and kissed her back."

"You sly old dog. You've still got the goods."

Buck shook his head. "I let it get out of hand when I should have stopped it."

"Why? You're a man. She's a woman. Neither one of you are attached to anyone else. If the chemistry is there—"

"She's a lovely girl, and damn, she needs somebody looking out for her—"

"She's a woman, Buck. Not a girl." Rufus was defending Chelsea, too. As irritating as it was to have his former partner playing devil's advocate right now, he was glad to know Chelsea had friends in her corner here at the lab. "Last I checked, you're both consenting adults. I'm a year older than you, and I'm not close to being over the hill. The age difference doesn't matter if that's what's holding you back."

But it did matter. Was he the only one who saw the problem here? Buck lowered his voice and leaned over the table. "The last thing I want is for her to confuse gratitude with lust or attraction. You know what Hunt did to her."

Rufus's teasing grin finally disappeared. "You mean that scumsucker who harassed every woman in this place before Lexi finally got him fired? You think you remind her of Hunt? No way. She'd avoid you like the plague if that was the case."

"He put his hands on her, Rufe." Buck's blood boiled to think of the violence and violation Chelsea had confessed to him last December. She'd cried in his arms for nearly twenty minutes before he'd been able to pull the story out of her. The idea that he could remind her in any way of the things Hunt had done was reason enough to avoid getting involved with her. "The same thing happened when she was a foster kid. She's got no reason to trust an older man."

"I would think that kind of abuse might keep her from trusting *any* man. But she seems to like *you*." Rufus leaned in, lowering his voice, too. "Have you given her any reason to distrust you?"

"Of course not."

"Then I don't see what the problem is." Rufus sat back, spreading his arms as if he was challenging him. "Come on, Buck—you're the biggest protector I've ever met. It's not in you to hurt that woman. Why do you think Bobby's disappearance is eating you up? Because you feel like you didn't protect him. I always felt safe knowing you had my back." He gestured to the lab hallway behind him. "One of the reasons I moved to admin after you left the force was because I couldn't trust another partner out on the streets the way I trusted you."

"That was work. This is personal."

"You need to get personal with someone." Rufus was on a roll. Whatever mood Buck was projecting this morning seemed to make his former partner think Buck needed an intervention. "Mary left you three years ago. And the marriage was rocky even before Bobby's disappearance. It's okay if you find somebody else."

"Not Chels."

Rufus threw up his hands. "Why not? In three years, I haven't seen you interested in anyone. Not until her."

"She's...different." Rufus's skeptical expression demanded an explanation. "Unique doesn't even begin to describe her. She's this center of goodness and light in the dark storm of life you and I see every day. And she doesn't even know it. She's impractical and disorganized. Brilliant and scatterbrained. She's not like Mary."

"That's a good thing. Mary divorced your ass. She wasn't tough. She couldn't roll with the punches life was throwing at you two."

Buck had thought this was a chance to vent to a friend, to back up his decision about curtailing a relationship with Chelsea. But Rufus seemed to be doing his damnedest to push him into one. "I'm not an easy man to be with."

"That's Mary talking. Chelsea *is* different. She's a survivor. She's testifying against the man who assaulted her. She's got her thumb in every case this lab works on. And she's not afraid to go toe to toe with you. She doesn't need easy—she needs reliable."

While Buck admired her persistence for her job or a cause she believed in, it also put her in harm's way. "She's a hazard to herself."

"All the more reason why she needs someone like you in her life. Let her shine and do her thing while you back her up. Give her a safe place to land in the middle of that storm when Hunt and the rest of the world are too much for her. From what I can see, she's good for you, too." He nodded to the mug on the table between them. "She pays attention to your needs and looks out for you. Makes you care about something besides finding your son. You're socializing again." Rufus arched a knowing eyebrow. "We all know about those breakfast dates you two have been having for months now."

"They're business meetings."

"Maybe they started out that way. Maybe that's the excuse you need to keep seeing her. But you've smiled around her more that you have in ages. Yeah, she marches to the beat of her own drum. She's the smartest person here, and that's saying something. She's got a big heart. Never forgets a birthday or special occasion. Always worried about others. Despite that crap she went through with Hunt as her supervisor, it didn't dim her light one bit." Rufus's tone finally softened. "She'd be good for an old curmudgeon like you."

Old curmudgeon? Buck swore at his partner's sarcasm and crossed his arms over his chest. "I thought you were trying to convince me I *wasn't* too old for her."

"You're not, you thickheaded mule. Bottom line. You like being with her?" Of course, he liked spending time with her. It wasn't exactly a chore to spend time with a woman who was funny, intelligent and sweet. "That kiss? Was it any good?"

"Do I ask you about your and Lakeisha's love life?"

Rufus whistled. "*Love life*, huh? It was that good?"

Yeah. Being with Chelsea made him feel good. Eating pancakes. Touching. Talking. He'd wanted to set her up on the kitchen counter and shove himself between her legs and take that kiss to a whole other level. It was the imprint of his manhood throbbing against his zipper, eager to get close to her heat, that had finally knocked some sense into his head and convinced him to pull away. "I don't want to be the next guy who hurts her."

"Then don't be. Be the guy who makes her happy." Rufus sounded as though simply saying the words out loud could make them so. "Be the guy who makes it safe for her to be who she needs to be."

Buck shook his head. "What the hell would Chelsea see in somebody like me, except a bodyguard or father figure? That's not what I want in a relationship."

His partner smirked, as if Buck had made his point for him. "When you were with her—did it feel like she was kissing her daddy?"

"Don't be gross."

"Did it?"

With crystal clarity, Buck relived every moment of that kiss. The feel of his hands in her thick hair and her fiery mouth demanding a response from his, her needy hands tugging him to her. Hell, he was getting hard again just thinking about how eagerly she'd given herself over to him.

Buck was so screwed. He slowly shook his head.

"I didn't think so." Rufus slapped the tabletop and stood. "She could make you happy. If you decide you want to be." The grin faded and his friend's gaze narrowed as he studied Buck's tight expression. "Unless you think you don't deserve to be happy."

Chapter Nine

"Why doesn't Buck deserve to be happy?"

Buck's gaze swung to the open door as Chelsea stepped into the lounge. "Chels."

She hugged her laptop to her chest with one hand and held her phone to her ear with the other. But even as she wrapped up her conversation, her frown of concern was fixed squarely on him. "Of course I will, Detective," she spoke into the phone. "I'll copy you on everything I find."

"Chelsea—"

"Is it because you're grumpy?" She tucked her phone into the pocket of her slacks. "You're not. That's an act to keep people at arm's length and make them think you're tough. People who know you respect you, and those who don't are intimidated by you, anyway. Do you feel guilty about Bobby and think you have to pay some kind of penance? Everyone deserves to be happy. Maybe you more than anyone—"

"Take a breath." Buck crossed to Chelsea and brushed his fingers across her cheek and cupped her delicate jaw. He inhaled and slowly released his breath, watching her nostrils flare, once, twice, again, as she matched her breathing rhythm to his. Chelsea was clearly upset. But he wondered how much of the anxiety lining her hazel eyes was concern about what she'd overheard at the end of his conversation with Rufus, and how much had to do with that phone call or whatever it was she wanted to talk to him about. Rufus had been right about one thing. He wanted to make Chelsea's life safer, easier—not add more stress.

"Rufe is worried about me putting my personal life on hold until I find Bobby," Buck explained. "But I'm happy."

Happy enough. He had happy moments. Although it was a little alarming to realize most of those moments were when he was with her. When had that happened?

She didn't look like she believed him. "*Are* you putting your personal life on hold? Is that why that kiss freaked you out? I forced you out of your holding pattern?"

"Nothing's wrong." Ignoring the question and refusing to admit that he would *freak out* about anything, he released her. He wanted to move past this touchy-feely conversation that was too focused on him and get to a topic he could do something about. "You look tired this morning. You getting enough sleep?"

Chelsea arched an eyebrow above her glasses and looked to Rufus. "Does he always change the subject when you're talking about him?"

Rufus laughed out loud. "Preaching to the choir, sister. On that note, I'll leave you two alone. She's good. For. You." He mouthed the message to Buck before patting Chelsea's shoulder. "This guy gives you any trouble, let me know."

"I will."

"I'm not going to give her..." But Rufus was striding

down the hallway, chuckling every step of the way, as if he understood something Buck didn't. Swallowing his irritation, Buck turned his focus back to Chelsea. "You're done with Grayson?" She nodded, but still hung back, as if wary of being alone with him. That felt like a well-deserved stab to the heart. "You wanted to tell me something?"

Chelsea circled around him to the table and set her laptop down. Without sitting, she tapped on the control pad. He swore he saw a shiver ripple across her shoulders. Hell. There *was* something wrong. That frown dimple appeared on her forehead again. "Are you sure you're all right? I didn't cause whatever you and Rufus were arguing about?"

"We weren't arguing. Rufus and I are fine. *I'm* fine." Seeing his reassurances did little to ease the worry above Chelsea's eyes, Buck nodded toward the laptop. "Forget it. What did you need to tell me? Something to do with that phone call?"

"Partly. That was Detective Dixon following up on the report I sent him this morning. About this." She pointed to the files on her laptop. "I found Bobby's DNA in another case file."

"What?" Buck quickly moved in beside her to study the report on the screen. There were two crimes now attributed to his son? "A mugging near the Yankee Hill Road homeless shelter?" He skimmed the details. A transient had been assaulted in an alley. In addition to the man's injuries, personal items, including a blanket and the change he had on him, had allegedly been taken. No leads on the assault, beyond a suspicion of gang activity that hadn't panned out.

"I copied the original report where it says that unidentified DNA was found on the old refrigerator box where he sleeps. Now Bobby's name is there as a match." Chelsea shivered again, as if feeling a chill. "Why didn't it show up until this morning? The incident happened back in February. It's like someone is plugging names into the system."

"I have a hard time believing anyone could hack into the crime lab's computer systems and plant my son's name. I have a harder time believing Bobby is committing these violent crimes."

"This doesn't feel like good news to me." Chelsea rubbed her hands up and down her arms. "Could Bobby be homeless? It's a hundred percent harder to track down someone living off the grid. They're invisible to most people and technology. It'd be a good way to stay off anyone's radar—if that's what he wanted."

Had Bobby been living on the streets of Kansas City, right under Buck's nose? It was a dangerous, unhealthy way to live for most people—and if Bobby was in that kind of trouble, why wouldn't he reach out to him for help?

But no matter how desperate Bobby might be, Buck couldn't believe that his son would assault a homeless drunk for some spare change any more than he'd murder a man. Still, if Bobby had been living in that alley, could someone have assaulted him, as well? Buck's heart was weary with the helplessness he felt.

"Why would he need to stay off the radar?" Buck tried to think of this like a cop, not a father—not only to focus on finding the answers he needed, but to cope with the ongoing worry. He understood Chelsea being perplexed by the unexpected clue. "It doesn't make sense to me, either. These two crimes are incredibly different. Clearly, the victims come from a different socioeconomic status. Two different parts of town. One was executed like a professional hit, and the other was a street scuffle with a broken nose and less than twenty dollars of property taken. How can they possibly be related?"

"I thought the differences were curious, too." She nodded to the screen. "The DNA was on the box this time, not the victim."

But it was still a lead Buck could explore.

"The Yankee Hill Shelter isn't that far from Sin City. I wonder if…" he squinted to read the victim's name "…Gerald Vaughn is still around for questioning. Maybe he'd recognize a picture of Bobby. If he'll talk to me. I'm guessing a homeless guy with substance abuse issues isn't going to have a friendly track record with cops."

"You're not a cop anymore," she pointed out. Buck gave her a fraction of the authoritative glare he'd put to good use for over twenty years. Chelsea arched her brows, sighing with understanding. "But you still look and act like one." She clicked off the dual file screens. "*I* could talk to him."

"No."

"But I'm not threatening."

Hence, the problem.

"No," he repeated more firmly.

"I know the director of the shelter. Tess Washington." Buck knew he didn't want to hear this explanation. "I stayed there a few times growing up. She might know Gerald. Or she could even know Bobby if he was ever a resident there. Since Vinnie has closed the bar until tomorrow night, I can stop by there this evening after work."

"Chels." He laid his hand over hers again. "I'm already uncomfortable with you being in that part of town. You could have been killed, remember?"

He felt her skin chill beneath his touch before she slipped her hand from beneath his. "I think we—I—have bigger problems than a random shooting at Sin City."

Although he didn't believe there was anything random about the shooting, Buck's senses sharpened. "Explain."

She pulled up her email. "This was in my inbox this morning. It's not the first one I've received. I haven't figured out what it connects to yet. I do so much work online. I tried to track down the source, but I need more time."

"You don't know who it's from?"

She shook her head.

"Is it spam?"

"No. This is…personal." Chelsea clicked on a message and nodded toward the screen, even as she hugged her arms around her waist and stepped back from the laptop. She retreated until her back bumped into his chest. But when she would have scooted aside, he closed his hands around her upper arms and felt her trembling. "I think it's related to that note that was on my car."

Buck read the message over her shoulder and cursed.

I warned you, bitch.

Which would be more painful for you? I can make anything happen online. Advertise a pair of bait dogs? Delete evidence files?

Stay out of my business.

The message was followed by two memes that would have turned a weaker woman into a quivering mess. In one, there was a cartoon picture of a dog hanging from a noose with a crude caption about peeing in the wrong yard. The other image was a newspaper photograph of Dennis Hunt from last year. Only, instead of the article announcing his arrest, it bore a computer-generated headline that read *All Charges Dismissed. Boo-hoo for His Victims*.

Buck read through the entire message three times, feeling his blood simmer into a boil at the unmistakable threat. He glanced at the sender's address. *Trouble@ haha.com*. Even that looked menacing. "How many of these messages have you received?" She clicked on a folder she'd dubiously named *Hate Mail*. When he saw the rows after rows of emails saved there, Buck cursed. "Is this why you texted me the other night? Damn it, Chels. You shouldn't have been alone. You should have told me about these threats. I would have come right back."

She turned to face him, tilting her gaze to his. "Would you? I wasn't sure. Things got weird between us." Even in that gentle tone, she didn't mince words. "I don't like it when you and I fight."

"It wasn't a fight, Chels." He hated the shadows of doubt that turned her hazel eyes a muddy color. "You caught me off guard with that kiss. I needed to work through some things."

"Felt like a fight to me."

He rubbed his hands up and down her arms, willing the shivering he felt to stop. "For that, I'm sorry."

Her eyes widened at his apology. "I thought you didn't—"

"You're right. Sometimes, there are things that do require an apology. Like me hurting you." Her ponytail hung over her shoulder. Buck caught its soft, heavy weight between his fingers before smoothing it down her back. "That was never my intention."

Gold and green sharpened in her eyes again. Then she stunned him by offering him a shy smile he didn't deserve.

She'd been scared and he hadn't picked up on her fear because he'd been too caught up in his own emotions. Then he'd avoided her by dropping her off at the lab and going back to work yesterday. He wasn't going to let her down like that again. "Any idea who this *Trouble* is? What business he's talking about?"

Her smile didn't last. Chelsea shook her head. "I'm guessing *Trouble* is his hacker name, but he's nobody I know in the online world. And it's not a person of interest in any of the cases I've been researching. I tried to trace his IP address. He was bouncing his signal all over the country, but it originated right here in the KC area. Although he hit a kill switch when I was getting close, and the trail went dead. If I'd stuck with it, I might have found his location. If he's online, that is. Last night I dozed off at my computer. And then I had to come to work. Plus, I can't do that kind of deep web search here at the lab because it's state equipment and I don't have a court order. The timing is circumspect, too." She pointed to a file icon labeled *Huh?* on her screen. "I've had more DNA matches pop up on cold cases—not all Bobby's," she assured him. "One of these cases is over a decade old, back when the Meade mob family still had some power in this town. An unsolved rape? A B&E at a tech firm?"

Buck frowned at the possibility that getting breaks on all these cases might not be a good thing. "Isn't that what your program does? Connect unsolved crimes to new DNA evidence? As more and more people are doing genealogy searches and online medical tests and that kind of thing?"

"Yeah, but…" She shook her head. "I'm good. But this is Las-Vegas-hit-the-jackpot lucky. I expected to get a couple of hits when I programmed my deep-dive alignment of database searches. But this is seventeen hits in one forty-eight-hour period. I'm ninety-nine percent certain we're dealing with a hacker—not your son going on a crime spree. I think *Trouble* is mad at me because in my search for Bobby, I tapped into whatever he's doing."

"What, exactly, is he doing?"

"I believe he's manipulating data—inserting false information into police investigations—to mislead detectives—eliminating suspects, sending them after a perp who doesn't even exist?"

"Like Bobby."

She nodded. "If I was a criminal, I'd love to see someone else's name attached to my DNA. *Trouble* could be doing it for grins and giggles—some hackers love to show how they can beat any system. Or, he could be doing it for profit."

"Criminals pay him to mislabel their DNA at a crime scene as someone else's."

She exhaled a weary sigh. "I haven't found proof yet to determine if it's strictly a cybercrime or if he's an accomplice to everything from a mugging to the murder of Yuri Dubrovnik."

"But you *can* prove something like that? Whether this *Trouble* is a cover-up for hire or a hacker with ego issues?"

"If I can find the money trail linked to the data manipulation," she answered modestly, as if anyone could master the kind of brainy tech magic she did. "Or I could bait him into making a mistake and prove he's not as good as he thinks he is."

Buck didn't like the sound of Chelsea and bait in the same sentence. He might not understand the how-to of the cyber scheme she was describing, but he understood the fear and frustration she was feeling in the way she was hugging herself and rambling on. The shadows beneath her eyes told him she hadn't gotten enough sleep to have the strength and mental clarity to deal with whatever this creep was threatening her with.

Be the guy who can make her happy. Be the guy who makes it safe for her to be who she needs to be.

Rufus's advice echoed inside his head. Buck reached up to free a long strand of hair that had caught beneath the earpiece of Chelsea's glasses. He tucked the strand behind her ear and let his fingers splay against the side of her neck. Her skin was cool to the touch, and he frowned, missing the vibrant energy that usually radiated from her. "Why didn't you tell me sooner? You must have been scared out of your mind."

"Scared, yes. But I could still think."

Bless her literal heart. "Did you get *any* sleep the last two nights?"

She braced her hand at the center of his chest. She pushed weakly against him, then curled her fingers into the front of his shirt, holding on. "Not much. I... He knows about Dennis. That's my private trauma... He threatened my babies..."

"Come here." When she swayed as if debating whether to latch on to his strength or stand on her own two feet, Buck made the decision for her. He slid his fingers beneath the base of her ponytail and palmed the small of her back with the other hand, pulling her into his body and holding her until her stiff arms between them relaxed. With a weary sigh, she gave up any resistance to his embrace and wound her arms around his waist. She tucked her forehead into the juncture of his neck and shoulder and leaned against him.

"He's ruining the crime lab's reputation, putting who knows how many investigations and prosecutions in jeopardy. I have to stop him."

"Easy, sweetheart. You don't need all the answers right now. Just rest a minute." Something inside Buck eased, as well, as she surrendered her weight to him for a few moments. "You're not in this fight by yourself." He had no respect for a man who gave himself a cutesy nickname and threatened the woman Buck cared about through the anonymity of the internet. "I'm sorry I wasn't there for you when you were being bombarded with these messages. But I'm here now. I've got you."

She inhaled a deep breath, and when she exhaled, she sank further into him. They were pressed together from shoulder to thigh, and Buck was more than aware of her nipples beading up between them and her fingertips clutching against his spine. Even though his body hummed at every point of contact, he concentrated on the uneven gusts of her breath against his neck and the nervous stroking of her fingers. He knew her brain was going ninety miles a minute, trying to process the threats and her emotional reactions to them. "I don't know how this happened, Buck. Computers are what I'm good at. I admit that I don't have good situational awareness—that I won't always see the guy in the alley with the gun. And I'm not very good at reading people—like my old boss asking me for a favor when he's really after something else. But cyberspace is my territory. It's where I'm the badass. My team needs me to figure this out. Bobby needs me to be as diligent and resourceful as I can be."

"No one doubts your skills."

"Yeah? *Trouble* got through firewalls and filters set up by the crime lab's so-called expert. And if he's the one who fired those shots at us, then he's also found a way to track me in the real world."

"Maybe it's not the same guy," Buck suggested, although he loathed the coincidence of a threat coming at Chelsea on two different fronts. With the kind of work she did, along with Hunt's upcoming trial, the double threat wasn't as impossible as he'd like it to be.

"No one should be able to get to me online. Why do you think I spend so much time with my computers? That's my safe place."

"*I'm* your safe place," he insisted, wishing he could make her believe there was so much more to her than her technical knowledge. Now that he knew she needed him, and seemed willing to accept his help, he dipped his nose to the fresh, lemony fragrance of her hair, surrounding her as tightly as he could in his embrace. "You'll get this *Trouble*," he whispered against her ear. "I know you will."

"How did he get through all my security? How did

he find me? I know it sounds arrogant, but I'm one of the best. How did he outsmart me?"

With his fingers tangled in the velvety thickness of her hair, he massaged her scalp. "He got lucky. You were exhausted and off your game because of the trial and the gunshots and maybe because of me. But you *are* the best. Never doubt that. He won't get lucky again."

Chelsea tilted her head back into the cup of his hand and raised her gaze to his. "You have that much faith in me?"

"Yeah. I do."

This time, her smile reached her eyes before she snuggled in again. "I'm not used to having someone in my corner."

"Well, you got me now. And I take up a lot of space in that corner."

She snickered. "As long as there's room for me."

"Always." Yeah. There would always be a place for her in his life.

"You give the finest hugs, Buck. I've never felt as secure or grounded as when you hold me." She slipped her thumbs through the belt loop at the back of his slacks, and her contented sigh tickled his skin and vibrated through him. "You smell good and you're toasty warm."

He never felt so good, so needed, so powerful as when she trusted him to hold her like this. Yeah, he could admit that he wanted more with Chels. Hell, he wanted everything a grown man could want. But this was good, too. Holding Chelsea calmed something inside him. Strengthened him.

Made him happy.

But it still pissed him off that she'd been threatened, and she hadn't believed it was okay to tell him about it.

Buck leaned back, framing her jaw between his big hands and tipping her face up, waiting until her gaze met his. "Here's the deal. From here on out—you get another threat, somebody creeps you out, you're in a situation and something seems off to you—you call me. Or text. Do not hesitate or second-guess my reaction. Do not dismiss what you're feeling. I'd rather you be wrong and safe than right and on your own." He traced the curve of her cheek with his thumb, locking his gaze onto hers. "Can you promise me that? I don't want you facing this *Trouble* guy alone. Even if it's online."

Her smile had faded, but she nodded.

"Say the words, Chels. I need to hear you're doing everything you can to keep yourself safe."

Those beautiful eyes never left his. "If I feel threatened or creeped out by something, I'll call or text for help."

His chest expanded with a sigh of relief, and he tilted her face in to press a kiss to her forehead. He lingered there until he felt her skin warm beneath his lips, until he felt her hands tighten into fists at the back of his waist. "Thank you."

The glimmer of a smile softened her lips as he pulled away. "You're easy to please."

"No, I'm not. I'm bossy as hell. I just gave an order when I should have asked. But I'm not apologizing. I need you to understand how important your well-being is to me." He slid his hands down the long column of her neck to grasp her shoulders again. "I'm not going to let my hang-ups or another misunderstanding come between us. I'm here for you. I have your best interests at heart. Do you have time to go home and take a nap after work?"

Her grip loosened on his back, and she frowned in confusion. "You want me to take a nap?"

He needed to find a way to explain his plans so that he didn't sound quite so much like a father figure. "Am I going to be able to talk you out of helping Vinnie at Sin City tomorrow night?"

"No."

"And your plans for tonight?"

"I thought I'd talk to my friend Tess at the shelter."

He released her entirely when she shifted away to close her computer. "You can't keep going without decent sleep. You've had a lot of stress. I'll take you home after work. No computers. You go to bed for an hour or so, while I take care of some things at the office. Then I'll bring takeout and we'll have dinner before *I* drive you to the shelter."

She rolled her eyes. "Yeah. I hear the *bossy* thing now."

"Please. I need to take care of you."

"Old-school alpha male?" She hugged her laptop to her chest, and it felt like she'd raised a shield between them.

"It makes me crazy when I think you're not safe," he admitted.

She studied his expression for a moment. "Okay."

"Okay? Just like that?"

"I can't have you coming apart on me," she teased. She squeezed his arm as she walked past him. "I'd better get back to my computers. I'll see you after work."

"I'll be here."

"Buck?" She paused in the doorway and looked back at him. "Can you do that accent thing again?"

There it was. Almost shy at first, then softening her whole face and lighting up her eyes. Chelsea smiled at him, and Buck felt like all the mistakes he'd made had been forgiven, and his world had righted on its axis again. He dredged up his best Scottish brogue and bowed his head. "Happy to be of service, mum. Your chariot will be waiting."

"Sexy as all get-out." A healthy shade of pink blossomed on her cheeks. "Thank you for caring, Buck. I haven't had much of that in my life. It feels…good." Her smile lasted until she turned and headed down the hallway toward her lab.

Rufus was right.

He *was* in love with her.

Chapter Ten

Chelsea managed to get a full hour of sleep before the nightmares started. She thrashed enough to twist the comforter around her legs and accidentally kick Peanut Butter, who was curled up in the crook behind her knees, out of his spot. The hissing cat had awakened Donatello and Raphael, and now the two poodles had their front paws propped up on the edge of the mattress, watching and sniffing with concern. And when Jelly howled from her perch on the shelf above the shaking headboard, the fully roused menagerie demanded petting, treats, an outing and reassurances that their stable home would continue to their satisfaction, despite Mama's little unconscious freak-out.

"So much for napping." Rolling over onto her back, she stared up into Jelly's green eyes on the shelf above her. "Fine. You all need some Mom time before I leave again."

Seeming satisfied with her response, Jelly hopped down and allowed Chelsea to trail a hand along the standoffish cat's back before she disappeared into another one of her hiding places behind the couch in the living room. Peanut Butter returned to the bed and claimed Chelsea's lap as she sat up, enjoying some cuddles before the two age-defying poodles running in circles and thumping their paws against the bed told her in no uncertain terms that they wanted her attention, too.

Her heart swelling at her fur babies' unique antics, Chelsea pushed back the covers and swung her legs over the edge of the bed. She still wore her blouse and slacks from work, and since pets didn't care about wrinkled clothes, she slipped on her shoes and grabbed her sweater from the foot of the bed. "Outside?" she teased, entertained by the dogs falling all over themselves with excitement at the possibility of a walk around the block and a chance to explore their territory again. She scratched around Raphael and Donatello's soft ears before grabbing her keys and heading to the back porch where she stored their harnesses, sweaters and leashes.

"Sit." Even though their tails never stopped wagging, both dogs dutifully obeyed and let her put their gear on. "Good boys." She petted them both and led them to the door before pulling on her vintage red wool coat that fitted at the waist and flared at the bottom. It wasn't as warm as the thrift shop men's coat she'd been wearing the night of the shooting, but she didn't plan to be outside for too long. She called to the cats before locking the house behind her. "PB and J? You guard the place. Mama and the boys will be right back."

Since it was still daylight, she felt safe enough walking the dogs. She lived in an older neighborhood, but the small homes were well taken care of. And with a church and its empty parking lot taking up most of the block across the street, there were no dark alleys where a shooter could hide. No strange houses where she hadn't at least met the residents.

She knew she could use a lot more sleep—whatever she was getting was interrupted by images of vile words and emoticons that turned into the faces of her friends and pets and floated across a computer screen like targets in a shooting gallery before the percussive attack of gunfire filled them with holes. But she felt more energized than she had all day. Her renewed sense of well-being had a lot to do with the healing power of her pets, but it also had to do with the fact that Buck had seen her safely home and inspected every door and window to make sure her place was secure before he ordered her to lie down and rest. She'd dozed off after he'd left, knowing he'd be back soon. The calming sense of security he brought to her life warred with the anticipation of seeing him again. But both were positive feelings that made her feel like she might finally have found the stability and normalcy that had long been missing from her life.

She needed Buck in the short term, to protect her from the threats she'd received. But she couldn't help thinking long-term thoughts about the man. She hadn't realized how sexy it was for a man to be mature, to be confident, yet not cocky, comfortable in his own skin, to have enough life experience under his belt to understand and do battle with the chaos that was her life. His silver-and-brown beard scruff gave his squarish features an extra layer of masculinity that tapped into every feminine cell of her body. His solid arms and broad chest provided a secure haven. She treasured every touch, every gruff, honest word. She loved making him smile. Loved working with him to find his son, loved the way he treated her as a valued partner in his quest.

She loved him, period.

Robert Buckner wasn't who she thought she would have such deep, complex feelings for—not in a million years. But now she understood why she hadn't found this kind of banked passion, simmering beneath the surface of every touch—why she hadn't found this unshakable trust with another man before. It was because she hadn't known Buck.

Now she had to make him believe that what she felt for him was real, not a schoolgirl infatuation or a victim attaching herself to the hero who'd rescued her. What they'd shared in that kiss was what she wanted in a relationship. Chemistry plus that depth of feeling was a balanced equation in her book. But Buck had fought so hard against it afterward, despite his apology at the lab, that she wasn't sure if anything beyond their friendship was even possible. But she wanted more.

More conversations. More smiles. More hugs. More kisses. More Buck.

Consumed by her thoughts, Chelsea waited as Donatello and Raphael sniffed their way around a stump at the edge of the parking lot, each raising their leg to shoot some fumes at one of their favorite stops. Since they were almost home, both dogs had long since run out of the means to stake out their territory. Giving the dogs their exercise and the secure life that had been missing from their early years gave Chelsea a sense of purpose. And her little pack gave her the same sense of belonging and stability that her rescue pets got from her.

"Come on, boys." She tugged on their leashes and

urged them into step beside her. Raphael heeled as he'd been taught, and Donatello rested his muzzle against his brother's shoulder, following them safely across the street to her driveway. "As soon as we get inside, we'll have treats—"

Chelsea startled at the roar of an engine revving nearby. She stumbled over the dogs' leashes as she whipped around to see a man on a motorcycle rolling up to the end of her driveway. Was this the man who'd shot at her? Threatened her? She no longer had the pictures from the security camera feed at Sin City to compare him to, but those images weren't ones she would soon forget.

Was this *Trouble*?

She instinctively backed away, then froze. Even with his helmet on, she recognized the man. "Oh, hell no."

"You get another threat, somebody creeps you out, you're in a situation and something seems off to you— you call me."

Buck's warning echoed in her head. This visitor definitely qualified for the creep factor. The man wasn't armed that she could see, but she didn't hesitate to pull her phone from her pocket. She pulled up Buck's number as the rider shut off the engine and nudged the kickstand into place. She typed out a brief message and hurried toward the side porch door. Raphael danced with excitement at their visitor, but Donatello, sensing something was amiss, tugged at his leash, growling as Dennis Hunt climbed off his bike. Chelsea tugged right back. "Come on, boys. We're going inside."

"Chelsea, wait. I don't want to cause any trouble."
Trouble? Poor choice of words, buddy. Her former

boss at the crime lab removed his helmet and set it on his bike. "I need your help."

Chelsea paused at the unexpected request. "No." A familiar loathing crawled across her skin as he stepped toward her. "You need to leave."

He closed the gap between them but stopped and put his hands up when Donatello lunged at him. The little dog couldn't even see the enemy, but he must be picking up on the distress flowing down the leash from her. Raphael joined the bark fest, forcing Dennis to raise his voice. "I know you have a big heart. You've forgiven a lot of people a lot of things."

He wanted forgiveness?

Dennis's dark blond hair had filled in from the hair plugs he'd gotten last year when he'd been wreaking havoc on her life, when he'd been in control of her job and blackmailing her into silence about the assault in his office. He was everything Buck wasn't. Arrogant. Self-centered. Dishonest. Even with the haggard expression shading his brown eyes, and his hands held up in a placating gesture, she couldn't drum up any sympathy for whatever his problem might be. Not for the first time, she wondered how far things would have gone that day if she hadn't grabbed the letter opener off his desk and defended herself. "You shouldn't be here."

"Call off your dogs." He huffed a breath of impatience, then offered what she supposed was meant to be a charming smile. "I just want to talk."

"My dogs are doing their job. You're not welcome here." She'd already sent the text, but she wasn't safe. Feeling her heart rate fire up with the telltale sign of a panic attack, she tapped Buck's number and put the phone to her ear. "You hurt me, Dennis. I don't think you understand the damage you did to me."

"Talking isn't going to hurt you," he insisted. "I need you to listen for two minutes before you call the cops."

Deciding the noisy poodles who didn't even reach his knees were no threat, he stepped between them and kicked, separating the brothers and tromping on one of their paws. Chelsea felt the dog's protesting yelp like a slap in the face. "Dennis!"

He snatched the phone from her hand and ended the call before tossing it into the snow behind him. "My fiancée, Roberta—she's threatening to leave me if I get convicted."

Chelsea picked up the dogs and retreated as far as the bottom step of the porch let her. Not that a blind dog and his clueless brother provided much of a shield, but at least Donatello kept growling and snapping at her former boss. "You had to know there would be consequences to your actions."

"I don't want to lose her," he argued, taking another step.

She glanced up at the side door, debating whether it was safer to have this confrontation out here, or if she could unlock the door, get inside and lock it behind her without him storming in after her. Although no one was driving or walking by her house at the moment, there'd definitely be no one to witness anything that happened if he got inside the house with her, so Chelsea planted her feet. "You should have thought of that before you put your hands on me."

"We're both adults." He glanced to one side, searching for his next words. "I was attracted to you. I hit on you. I thought you were interested."

A half dozen curse words, none of them ladylike, calling him on the bald-faced lie danced on her tongue. But he wasn't worth uttering them. She might have gotten the worst of his attention when he'd worked at the crime lab because she'd seemed the most vulnerable, but she wasn't the only woman he'd harassed there. "You're making excuses. That harassment was a power trip for you. You were our supervisor. You were supposed to protect us, not blackmail us into silence. As for groping me?—hurting me? I had bruises for weeks. No woman is interested in that. And don't touch my dogs again."

"I'm trying to salvage my career," he pleaded. "My whole life is going down the toilet because of you. I'm not saying I was a choir boy. But can't I change your mind about testifying to a lesser offense?"

"No."

With a nod of resignation, he put up his hands as if surrendering, and backed away. Willing the pulse pounding in her ears to calm enough to think, she decided her phone was too far away—too close to Dennis's motorcycle—to safely retrieve. Instead, she pulled her keys from her pocket and risked turning to insert her key into the lock.

Then a whole cluster of things happened all at once. The dogs growled. Dennis clamped his hand over her arm and yanked her around to face him. She lost her grip on the dogs and dropped Raphael, who yelped. Whether defending his brother or defending her, Donatello snapped at Dennis and came back with a chunk of skin from his finger. She heard the screech of tires braking across the pavement.

"Stupid mutt!"

When he pulled back his bloodied finger to backhand either her or the dog, Chelsea jerked back and tripped on the step, landing on her butt on the porch. His blow missed and she tumbled free of his grasp. But now he was leaning over her, and she had nowhere left to retreat. She kicked out, connecting with his shin, their positions feeling sickeningly familiar. "Go away!"

After her first blow, he dodged her feet and kept coming. "I know you have a heart, Chelsea. You care when people are suffering. Look at me. I'm a wreck." Donatello snarled in her lap. Raphael barked. "Shut them up!"

Dennis yanked their leashes from her fingers, winding them around his hand. "What are you...?" Despite Chelsea sitting up and scrambling to retrieve her precious babies, he jerked their leashes up until both dogs were dangling from his grasp. Donatello and Raphael twisted in the air, struggling against their nooses, whining in panic. When he cocked his arm to sling the dogs away from him, she screamed. "No!"

A shadow loomed up behind Dennis. A fist came down on his forearm, knocking his grip open and dropping the dogs into Chelsea's lap.

"Keep your hands off her!" Buck's blessedly deep, angry voice reached her ears even before she saw his face or recognized the broad shoulders behind Dennis.

Dennis seemed to fly through the air. But even as she caught the dogs' leashes and stooped between them to make sure they were all right, she realized Dennis wasn't flying—he was caught in Buck's powerful grip. Dennis's protests became a gasp of pain as Buck twisted his arm behind his back and shoved him to the ground with his knee in Dennis's back.

"Get inside," Buck ordered, turning his mouth to the shoulder of his insulated jacket without taking his eyes off Dennis. Understanding who was the protection expert here, Chelsea pushed to her feet and turned her key in the lock. But Buck's terse words to Dennis carried loudly and clearly behind her. "When I let go, you're going to get on your motorcycle and ride away, while you can still walk."

"You're threatening me?"

Chelsea felt a giggle in her throat at the idea of Dennis challenging Buck. She choked back the impulse, knowing it was nerves and not humor that made her want to laugh.

"I'm explaining the situation to you." Chelsea waited inside the screen door to watch Buck haul Dennis to his feet. Despite the blond man's struggles against the arm twisted behind his back, Buck didn't have any problem *guiding* him back to his bike. Buck released him and shoved his helmet into his gullet. Dennis folded with a loud *"Oof!"* but wisely stayed on his side of the motorcycle since Buck wasn't backing off. "You don't get to see Chelsea until you're in court," he warned. "You do not talk to her. You will not get close enough to threaten her again."

Dennis strapped on his helmet but risked a look beyond Buck's shoulder to the back door. "Hired yourself a real guard dog, I see."

Chelsea was shaking now, probably adrenaline crashing and leaving her body. She hugged Donatello and Raphael tighter to her chest. "Go away, Dennis."

Buck had changed from his regular uniform of a suit and tie into jeans, a T-shirt and his leather jacket, the casual look making him seem even more capable of handling himself in a fight with a scumbag like Dennis. "Chelsea's made her wishes clear. More than once. This time, I'll make sure you listen. Leave right now, Hunt. I'll be calling the DA's office to let them know you approached a witness who's testifying against you."

Dennis climbed on his bike and started the engine. "Stupid bitch. You're messin' up people's lives. Livin' in cyber land. You don't understand anything about the real world, do you?"

Chelsea cringed at the hateful words, but Buck didn't hesitate. He did some twisting thing and suddenly, Dennis was bent over his bike. The only thing that kept his face from being smashed against the handlebars was the helmet he wore. Buck leaned over him, his hushed words barely reaching Chelsea. "*You're* the one who doesn't understand. You touch her, her dogs, or her property again and I'm the one you'll be dealing with. You understand *that* reality?"

Dennis ground out a "Yes" between clenched teeth before Buck released him and backed away.

The former cop with the sprinkling of silver in his dark hair pulled out his phone and made a call while Dennis massaged his sore shoulder. When he sensed Buck's impatience, he muttered that he was leaving already and steered his motorcycle back into the street.

"Rufus." Buck reported the incident to his former partner while he watched Dennis turn the corner at the end of the block and disappear from view. Buck waited a few more minutes, probably to make sure Dennis wasn't circling around to pay her another visit, before he climbed behind the wheel of his idling truck and pulled into her driveway. He shut off the engine and climbed down, scooping up her phone from the snow as he talked to Rufus King. Buck's whiskey-brown gaze latched onto Chelsea through the screen door as he strode onto the porch. "He's still in one piece. He won't be the next time he touches her." Buck pulled open the screen door and stepped inside, forcing Chelsea to take several steps back while he locked the interior door and ended his conversation with his former partner. "Thanks. I owe you one." He dropped her phone onto the table beside the door, then held out his phone in front of her face. "*This* is what you sent me? Do you have any idea how scared I was? How many traffic laws I broke getting here? I left our damn dinner in the takeout window of the restaurant. I had no idea what I was walking into."

Chelsea stared at the three little words that had spurred her warrior into action.

I need you.

Had she ever admitted that to any man? Had she ever believed anyone would answer? "You said you'd come running. You did."

"Ah, hell." When he saw how badly she was shaking, Buck pocketed his phone, then held his arms out wide. "You all right?"

Chelsea didn't hesitate for one second. She walked into Buck's chest and tucked her forehead into the junction of his neck and shoulder. He wound his arms around her, dogs and all, tunneling his fingers beneath the base of her ponytail and palming the back of her neck, cradling her head beneath his chin. She felt the tension in him dissipate as she relaxed against him, soaking in the warmth and security he provided.

"Sweetie, you've got to talk to me." His strong fingers massaged her scalp. "Did he hurt you?"

Chelsea shook her head, reveling in the way every raw emotion in her eased at the touch of his hand and the raspy demand in his voice. "I'm okay. Just...rattled."

"Me, too." His hand was almost rough against her skin, tugging her hair loose from its ponytail. "Rufus is calling the DA's office to report the incident. An officer will be paying Hunt a visit. And Kenna Parker-Watson, the assistant DA who's running the case against Hunt, will be contacting Hunt's attorney."

Chelsea burrowed into the scents of leather, soap and Buck himself. The man was such a rich experience for the senses—his smell, his touch, the rumbling bass of his voice. Add in physical strength, surprising tenderness and that air of authority? How could he think that she—or any woman, for that matter—wouldn't be attracted to him on a visceral level?

She was surprised at the stab of jealousy that shot through her at the thought there probably was another woman out there more suitable for Buck. Someone more mature, more grounded. Some normal woman who led a normal life. But his arms were around *her*. Those words and that strength were focused on *her*. Ignoring the dogs squirming between them, Chelsea curled her fingers into the soft cotton of his black T-shirt and the warm skin and muscles underneath, claiming this man for her own.

At least for as long as he was willing to let her cling to him.

Chelsea wasn't sure how many seconds, or maybe even minutes, passed before she became aware of the cold noses snuzzling her chin, and heard the eager lap of dog tongues rasping against the stubble on Buck's neck. A deep chuckle vibrated in Buck's throat at the dogs' insistence that this embrace needed to end. She was surprised when he scooped the dogs from her grasp as he stepped away. "Come on, dudes." Leaving their sweaters on, Buck unhooked their leashes and set Donatello and Raphael on the floor. They trotted away to the kitchen, their confrontation with Dennis seemingly forgotten. Buck settled one hand at the small of her back, urging her to follow the dogs. "I fully intended to feed you tonight. But I was desperate to get to you. Maybe we can make a donation to the shelter and eat dinner there instead?"

Chelsea handed out treats and praised the dogs. "I'm good with that. Let me pay for the dinner you lost, though. What do I owe you?"

"Just some answers." Buck shrugged out of his jacket and helped her with hers before draping them over the back of the chairs at the table. She wasn't surprised to learn Buck's attention was still on her run-in with Dennis. "What did Hunt want?"

She busied herself filling the dogs' water bowls so she wouldn't dwell on the fact that Dennis had gotten close enough to touch her again. The hard grasp on her arm today wasn't anywhere as painful or humiliating as what he'd done to her in his office the year before, but the ick factor—and the fear of things escalating to another sexual assault—had felt the same. "To go easy on him at the trial. He said I was ruining his engagement, that my accusations were unfounded. That I'd misinterpreted what happened between us."

Buck moved in beside her to wash his hands, purposely nudging her shoulder with his. "Hunt is a self-absorbed pissant. You know that, right?"

Chelsea caught her lip between her teeth, fighting off the tears that stung her eyes, and looked up into the warm intensity of Buck's whiskey-colored gaze. She nodded.

His gaze never wavered. "You told him *no* then, and you told him *no* today. Nothing about that is consensual."

"I know." She bumped his shoulder in return, loving his unflinching support. "But it's good to hear someone else say that."

"What were you doing out there in the first place? How did he get to you?"

Strengthened by his body heat seeping across the minuscule space between them, Chelsea answered. "The dogs needed to go out. It's still daylight. I figured I'd be safe. Dennis must have been watching for me. He zipped around the corner and pulled into the driveway the moment we got to the house. I barely got that text off to you before Dennis grabbed my phone."

His mouth tightened into a grim line at hearing Dennis had attempted to stop her from getting help. "I texted back, asking for details. I thought either you weren't able to talk, or you were second-guessing about asking for help. I know that in your own wacky, brilliant, big-hearted way, you've become a strong, independent woman. But I wasn't going to let you face any threat by yourself." He reached out to free the band that still clung to a section of her hair. He combed his fingers through the heavy waves before smoothing the long strands down behind her back. With his face still downcast, he tilted his gaze up to hers. "I'd miss our breakfasts if anything happened to you."

Chelsea lost herself in the deep brown and gold irises that seemed to blaze from the inside out, and felt her breath catch at the confession behind his words. She hadn't realized how lonely the heavy burden of surviving she'd been carrying her entire life was until that very moment, when Buck's strength and stability lifted that burden from her. "I wasn't second-guessing. I wanted you here," she admitted. "I'd miss our breakfasts, too. Thank you."

He ignored her thanks, as if rescuing damsels and dogs in distress was standard operating procedure for him. He stooped to run his hand around the ears and muzzles of the poodles who had curled up beside his foot as though they'd been waiting for an alpha male to take charge of their pack so they could relax their guard duties. They pushed their heads into the warm stroke of his hand. "I guess you needed a bigger bull-dog than these two fluff-balls."

Recalling every vivid sensation of Buck's fingers caressing her hair and the side of her cheek and neck with the same gentle authority, she defended her dogs. "They're small, but mighty. They did their best to protect me. Raphael barked the entire time until Dennis stepped on his paw. Donatello bit him. I suppose I should check him for rabies."

"Hunt?"

"Donatello."

Buck's rugged features softened as he chuckled. "Good job, men." After treating the dogs to full-blown tummy rubs, Buck straightened in front of her. He clasped her shoulders and leaned in to press a kiss to her forehead. His lips lingered there, near her hairline, until he exhaled a long breath that danced across her skin. "I'm just glad you're okay."

"Why do you do that? Kiss me on the forehead?" She frowned, shifting her glasses on the bridge of her nose. "I asked Lexi why a guy would do that. She said to talk to you. It makes me feel like a little girl. I don't feel like a little girl with you."

"That's not my intention, I assure you. I know we're both adults."

Keeping his distance wasn't about the difference in their ages? "Then why? Don't tell me you kiss all your friends that way. You don't kiss Rufus on the forehead," she teased, trying not to reveal how much his explanation meant to her.

That earned her another low-pitched chuckle. "Nope. I have never done that with Rufe."

Chelsea was so desperate for something more with Buck that she couldn't let the question drop. If he didn't see any chance at a relationship with her, she wanted to know now so that she could rein in any misguided hopes before she got her heart completely broken. "Is that how you kissed your wife?"

His eyebrows lifted at her question, perhaps finally understanding how important this was to her. "Sometimes. We didn't have much physical contact toward the end."

"But you're such a physical guy."

"Mary wasn't interested, and I was too distracted—obsessed—with Bobby's disappearance to do anything about it, so no, we weren't intimate or physical in any way." Buck's shoulders and chest expanded with a deep breath. "When I kissed you the other night, when I…

claimed you—that was the first time I let go like that in years." Even though her heart thumped in her chest at the idea that Buck had claimed her—his words—that he'd felt the same passionate connection she did—there must have been something in her expression that reflected her confusion. "Come here." He pulled out a chair from the table and sat, putting his gaze eye-level with hers. He tugged Chelsea in to stand between his thighs. At first, his hands settled at her waist and hers rested on his sturdy biceps. Chelsea held her breath. The intimacy of this position felt serious. But whether holding her like this was serious good or serious in a bad way remained to be seen. Then, as his beautiful eyes danced with a dozen unreadable emotions, he reached up and pushed her glasses into place. He drew his finger down the ridge of her nose before clasping her waist again. "It's a safe way for me to touch you. I mean, I had to sit here for a minute to get my impulses under control so we could have this conversation."

Safe? Not the answer she'd expected to hear. Distancing. Polite. Indifferent. But safe?

"Buck, I'm thirty-two. I know how things work between a man and a woman. I don't have a lot of experience, but I'm not a virgin. I like you. A lot. I think I've made that clear, haven't I? It's not like with Dennis. I don't want him to touch me again. Ever." Her teeth clicked together as she visibly shuddered at the memory of his assault. "But when you do, it's…different. It feels—"

"Comforting?" She felt his fingertips clench against her hips.

For the first time in her socially awkward brain, a realization clicked into place. She wasn't the only one who felt unsure about whatever this was between them. Buck had lost his son. His wife had rejected him. He'd retired from the job he'd loved and launched a new business. He might be mature in the best of ways, but he'd basically rebooted his life four years ago. Starting a relationship probably felt as strange and uncertain to him as it did to her. Big, bad Buck needed tenderness and reassurance, too. Chelsea squeezed his shoulders and tried to explain the things he made her feel. "When you hold me, I don't think of teddy bears. It's more like…" She smiled at the image that sprang to mind. "Like a caveman telling all the other Neanderthals and saber-toothed tigers that I'm protected. That I belong to you."

"Caveman?" The lines beside his eyes deepened, and he looked dubious about the flattery of her comparison.

"I'm not talking about your looks or your manners. It's more the primalness of it. When you hold me, I feel excited. Centered, yet off-kilter at the same time. I feel connected to you in a way I crave." Her fingertips strayed across the stubble of his jaw, and she stroked the pad of her thumb across his lips. She felt powerful, encouraged, seeing his eyes darken as his pupils dilated at her touch. "But I can handle more. I'm not afraid of you treating me the way a man treats a woman, of you losing control. I *want* that."

Buck pulled her into his arms again, resting his cheek against her chest as he held her close. "You don't know how relieved I am to hear you say you aren't threatened by my touch the way you were with Hunt." He loosened his grip on her enough to tilt his head back and look up into her eyes. "But it scares me, too. *You* scare me."

Aghast, Chelsea leaned back against his hands at her back. "*I* scare you?"

"The things you make me feel do." He captured a lock of hair between his fingers, dipped his nose to it and inhaled deeply, sighing before he tucked it back behind her ear. "I kiss you on the forehead because it gives me a taste of everything I want to do, everything I want to be, with you. It tides me over until you're ready for something more. Until I'm sure you think of me the same way I think of you."

"How do you think of me?"

"Like I wish I was thirteen years younger and there wasn't any emotional baggage between us that we have to deal with."

The hungry look in his eyes made it difficult to breathe. "Buck…"

"I want you. Make no mistake about that. But I'm not sure you really understand what that means. The thought of Hunt hurting you makes me livid. Knowing you're afraid of this *Trouble* guy guts me. I'm used to taking charge and fixing problems. I get the job done. I don't take nothing off nobody. Being that…intense… has already cost me a marriage to the woman I thought I'd be with for the rest of my life. I'm forty-five years old. I don't think I can change the core of who I am." His fingers pulsed around her waist again, as if he was waging an internal battle whether to pull her nearer or push her away. "You will always have my protection. I promise. But I don't do anything halfway, sweetheart. If I go all in with you…" Her breathing quickened right along with his, and when he paused, she held her breath. "If it doesn't work out between us, I don't know if there's any coming back from that. So, I'm being cautious. For your sake as well as mine."

There was a long pause as she studied the blend of pain, hope and raw honesty on his weathered face. Chelsea brought her hands up to either side of his neck and stroked her thumb along his stubbled jaw. "All of that's going on inside when you kiss my forehead?" He nodded. It seemed her take-charge guy had one significant vulnerability—entrusting his heart to anyone else. Chelsea vowed then and there to protect that vulnerability and keep Buck safe as much as she knew how. "Thank you for sharing that. A chaste kiss on the forehead is a secret code for 'you're feeling something really intense, but you don't want to hurt me or scare me away'?"

He chuckled at that, though his hard expression barely changed. "That's oversimplifying it. But yeah, something like that."

"Then kiss my forehead any time you want." She rested a hand over her heart. "And I'll feel it in here, knowing it means something more. Knowing the timing isn't right yet. But one day soon, I hope, it will be. Your secret is safe with me."

"That sounds a little mushy when you put it like that. I'm not the mushy type."

"Maybe not." The more she understood his reasons for being wary of going all in with her, the more certain Chelsea felt like this could work between them. She skimmed her fingers over the ticklish buzz cut of hair at his temple and touched her thumb to the bandaged cut on his cheek. "But I think you might be *my* type."

"You're into cavemen?"

"I'm into you," she admitted. "I don't mind *intense*. It's who you are. I get pretty intense, too, when I'm lost in my work. It takes someone special to see past my obsession to understand who I really am inside. I see you, too, Buck. The protector. The father. Relentless investigator. Big softie who spoils my pets. The silver fox who kisses so hot when he loses control that I can't think straight. The man who feels things more deeply than a casual observer might expect. I can handle your kind of *intense*."

"Chels—"

She pressed a finger over his lips to silence whatever argument he was about to make and pulled away. "I'd better get changed if you're taking me to the shelter. There's cold water in the fridge if you're thirsty. Or sodas. You could brew some coffee if you have to have it, although I don't think you need it."

He grinned at her ongoing efforts to take care of him. "No coffee, I promise. I'll be fine."

Stopping at the archway that led into the rest of the house, she eyed the dogs at his feet and grinned at the cats meowing from the back porch. "Would you mind feeding my menagerie, then? It'll save me a few minutes before we have to leave."

Buck nodded and pushed to his feet. "I can handle these guys. But get a move on it. I want to see if we can find Gerald Vaughn. Then, I'm getting you home early. You need some downtime. We both do."

Chelsea hesitated for a moment. Then she smiled. She walked straight back to Buck, cradled his face between her hands, then tilted his head down as she stretched up on tiptoe to press a kiss to his forehead. She lingered for a moment, the same way he had with her earlier. Then she smiled against his warm skin and released him before scuttling off to her bedroom to change.

She hoped he understood the secret message she was sending, too.

She loved him.

Chapter Eleven

Other than the bars over the first-floor windows, the Yankee Hill Road homeless shelter reminded Buck of a grand old church with its thick, redbrick walls, wide concrete steps and marble entryway. Inside, the layout was more like a college dormitory, with a check-in desk behind a glass partition, and offices flanked by a large common area on one side, and the kitchen and dining area, set with rows of folding chairs and tables, on the other. There were stairs and an elevator that led to the upper levels, which he assumed were the sleeping quarters for the staff residents and overnight guests.

After assurances that they weren't seeking accommodations, Buck and Chelsea had been shown through a locked gate back to the director's office. If Buck expected this to be a quick, businesslike interrogation into the whereabouts of Gerald Vaughn and whether or not anyone around here had seen Bobby, however, he was out of luck. The moment the resident assistant at the front desk had opened the director's door, the large Black woman inside, with thick gray braids wrapped around her head, clapped her hands, squealed in delight and pushed up out of her chair to hurry around her desk. "Chelsea, sweet girl. You come here."

"Tess!" Chelsea hurried to meet the older woman, and they swallowed each other up in a hug. Buck quietly closed the door behind them and stood back to give them time to greet each other. "It's good to see you."

The two women rocked from side to side for a few moments before the shelter director pulled away to frame Chelsea's face between her hands. The older woman frowned at something she saw in Chelsea's expression. "You're looking tired. Stressed. Please don't tell me you're back here to see ol' Tess because you're in trouble."

"I'm fine. Still working at the crime lab."

"Still helping Vinnie? I heard his place got shot up a couple nights ago."

"No one got seriously hurt." Chelsea glanced up at Buck, eyeing the bandage on his cheekbone, and he wondered if she was remembering how close those bullets had come to hitting them. "Vinnie closed for a couple of nights to move past the shock and clean up, but I'll be there for him when he reopens."

Tess clucked her tongue behind her teeth and pulled her hand away. "That old coot takes advantage of you."

"*That old coot,*" Chelsea mocked, "introduced me to you. He saved my life. So, I don't mind."

"Your heart's too big for your sense. Always has been. Help Vinnie do his taxes or build a website," she chided. "You don't need to be serving up drinks at that place."

While Sin City was hardly a website kind of establishment, Buck was relieved that someone else could see the danger that Chelsea's compassionate nature put her in. Even though she was the one who'd been victimized as a child, he wondered if her compulsion to rescue was a manifestation of post-traumatic stress or survivor's guilt. She hadn't saved her parents—could she save someone else? Or was she compelled to help others because no one had saved her when she needed it most? But even as he vowed to take Rufus's advice to heart and be the anchor she needed, Buck was equally impressed to see firsthand the connections Chelsea seemed to have all over the city, simply because she was that kind, caring woman. Whether it was on a computer or in person, he'd never had as much faith in another person to find the answers he needed.

The women both adjusted their glasses into place before Tess folded her arms beneath her ample bosom and looked beyond Chelsea's shoulder to Buck. "This your man?"

Buck watched Chelsea's cheeks color with a blush as she turned and reached back to pull him to her side. "Yes. This is Robert Buckner."

Buck inhaled to mask the feeling of his chest puffing out at Chelsea's words. He'd expected her to correct Tess Washington's assessment of their relationship, but Chelsea hadn't even hesitated to claim him as hers. He liked the feeling. Then again, maybe she was playing a ruse that would make him less threatening to the staff and visitors here at the shelter. He quickly squelched the sense of belonging that had surged through his veins and extended his hand. "Everyone calls me Buck, ma'am."

"I'm Tess."

Chelsea beamed a smile at the grandmotherly woman. "However, I am hoping you can help me..." She dragged her hand down Buck's forearm and laced her fingers together with his, including him in her request. "…help *us* find someone who's missing."

"Missing? I don't like hearing that." Tess invited them to sit before she circled around the desk to her own chair. "How can I help?"

Chelsea took a seat and pulled Buck into the chair beside her. "We're looking for a man named Gerald Vaughn."

Buck watched the older woman's demeanor change. He recognized the suspicion that stiffened her posture behind the desk. "Gerald's not missing. He's been a fixture around this part of the city for years. Who are you really looking for?"

Buck unlocked his phone and pulled up a high school graduation picture—sadly, the most recent photo he had of his son. "My son. Bobby."

"Robert Buckner, Jr.," Chelsea clarified. Her hand settled on Buck's thigh after he handed his phone across the desk. Even that light touch seemed to take away some of the rawness he felt when he considered everything that could have happened to his son, and the things he might have been forced to do to survive, these past four years. "He's about six-two. Brown hair, brown eyes. Although he could have changed his look. He'd be twenty-three now. He might also have a different name, changed his whole persona to avoid the law or some other trouble he might be in. He's a gay man if that helps him stand out for you in any way. He might have come through here with a partner."

Buck couldn't help but admire the slender woman with the gorgeous hair and intelligent hazel eyes seated beside him. Chelsea's entire brain worked like one of those complicated algorithms on her computers. She knew what questions to ask, what details to share, what connections to seize upon, to find the information he needed. He'd never understood how much of a turn-on brains and compassion could be until he'd opened his world—and his heart—to Chelsea. His vow to keep her safe suddenly didn't seem like enough to make up for everything she'd done for him these past several months.

"Losin' your boy. That's rough." Tess handed the phone back to him. "You think Bobby has been in my shelter? That Gerald knows him?"

Buck settled his hand over Chelsea's. He'd conducted plenty of interviews like this when he was a cop, but there were extra layers of guilt and fear he had to rein in when the at-risk individual was his own flesh and blood. But everything seemed a little easier, more manageable when he felt Chelsea's supportive touch. Hell. He was so in love with this woman, and he hadn't even realized it. His feelings for Chelsea had crept up on him. Seeing her nearly every day had become a personal need more than any kind of business necessity. Having her at his side right now as they closed in on the first leads they had into Bobby's disappearance made him stronger, more patient, and hopeful that she'd be there to celebrate with him—that he'd have a reason to celebrate—soon.

Squeezing Chelsea's hand beneath his, he calmly explained what had led them here. "Chelsea found evidence that puts Bobby at the scene of a crime committed against Mr. Vaughn in the alley outside."

"I've seen my fair share of young men doing what was necessary to survive on the streets. Life is pretty tough around here." She arched a gray eyebrow at Chelsea. "As you well know."

"I remember." Chelsea scooted forward in her chair without breaking contact with Buck's leg. "We'd like to talk to Gerald about the night he was assaulted. Does he ever come here for assistance?"

Tess sat back in her chair with a heavy sigh. "He won't stay with us—says our rooms are too confining. But he usually shows up for dinner."

"Do you mind if we wait to chat with him?" Chelsea asked.

Tess hesitated, "If your boy hurt Gerald, I'm not anxious to bring it up. Gerald has a unique relationship with reality, and I don't want to upset him."

Chelsea released Buck and leaned forward to grip the edge of the desk. "I don't believe he hurt Gerald. There's something off about that crime scene. And from all the research I've been doing for months, I can't believe Bobby would hurt anyone. Maybe he was a witness. Maybe he was living in the same alley. Maybe he was a victim, too, and chose not to report it."

"His daddy looks like he could hurt someone," Tess observed, turning her focus to Buck. "You a cop?"

"KCPD, retired, ma'am. Right now, I'm a worried father looking for his son."

The older woman considered his words for several moments before sitting back in her chair. "Cops make some of my friends nervous. You might fit in a little better if you lost that gun you're wearing and helped us serve dinner and clear tables. We can always use the extra hands around here."

Buck got the feeling that Tess Washington would make a formidable poker player. As welcoming and grandmotherly as her demeanor might be on the surface, he could guess that Tess didn't take crap from anyone, and that she'd be equally fierce about protecting anyone she cared about. When she unlocked the top right drawer of her desk, Buck stood and peeled off his jacket to shrug off his shoulder holster. "I'd be happy to volunteer." Chelsea rose beside him, slipping off her backpack and handing it over, as well, before shrugging out of her coat.

"I'm guessing Chels was already planning to help out."

The older woman laughed. "You know our girl well." Tess locked the drawer and showed that she was slipping the key into the pocket of her jeans, so that they could retrieve their property later. "All right. If Gerald is willing to speak with you, and you don't upset anyone else, we'd love to have you stay for a couple of hours."

"Thanks, Tess." The two women exchanged another hug before heading to the door. "Aprons still in the same place?"

"You know it." A quick knock at the door interrupted their exit. "Come in."

"Tess, the damn dishwasher is…" A young man in his mid- to late twenties pushed open the door but stopped midsentence when he saw Buck and Chelsea in the office. "Sorry. Didn't know you had a meeting."

Tess caught him by the elbow and linked her arm through his before he could back out of the office. "It's all right, Art. Come in. Let me guess, we'll be washing dishes by hand this weekend?"

"'Fraid so, ma'am."

"I'll call the repairman and see if he can get here

on Monday." With that problem sorted for now, Tess turned and smiled. "I want you to meet an old friend of mine. Art, this is Chelsea O'Brien. I've known her since she was a little girl."

"Nice to meet to you." Chelsea extended her hand.

The younger man was slow to take it and offered no polite words of greeting. But even as he shook Chelsea's hand, his dark eyes were focused on Buck. "And you?"

Buck thought he saw Tess squeezing the young man's arm, silently warning him to mind his manners. Or did that signal mean something else? Something about the young man's abrasive demeanor set off warning bells in Buck's head. "Robert Buckner. Nickname's Buck."

"Buck?" Buck rested a hand at the small of Chelsea's back and stepped closer to her, not liking the prickly vibe radiating off the other man. "Arthur Kendrick. Resident chef. Nickname's Art," he mimicked. "You a cop?"

"Used to be."

"Buck's a private investigator," Chelsea intervened, trying to ease the tension in the room. "I'm with the crime lab. We're working a missing person case."

Art was several inches shorter than Buck, and had a compact, wiry build. His long black hair was pinned up in one of those trendy man-buns at the back of his head. Sleeves of black tattoos going up each forearm emphasized sinewy muscles. Buck recognized some of the ink symbols and knew Art had spent time in a gang when he was younger. That could explain his distaste for an authority figure. "Missing person? That's your excuse for poking your noses into our business?"

"Arthur!" Tess visibly tugged on his tatted arm, cajoling him. "Be nice. I just recruited a couple of dishwashers for you tonight."

Art lowered his defiant gaze. "Appreciate the help."

Tess pushed him toward the door. "You run along now. Folks will be lining up. And be a dear and let me know when Gerald Vaughn comes in. Chelsea and Buck need to talk to him."

The younger man paused in the doorway and crossed his arms over his chest. "Why do you want to talk to Gerald? He's a little off in the head. Not violent or anything, but there's no telling what's going to come out of his mouth."

"You protective of him?" Buck challenged.

"I'm protective of everyone here." Although the scars on Art's fingers and knuckles could be from his time in the kitchen, or his time in a gang, it looked as if he was no stranger to a fight. "Yankee Hill's not only my job, it's my home."

Art drilled Tess with a warning look, and the hairs at the back of Buck's neck stood straight up. What was this guy's problem? His attitude made Buck think of the surly young drunk with the hoodie and the hooker at Sin City. With his threat radar on full alert, Buck slipped his arm around Chelsea's waist and tucked her to his side. She seemed to think there were answers at the shelter, but all he saw were people with secrets and suspicion in their eyes. He couldn't help but slide his gaze back to the desk where Tess had stashed his weapon. He wasn't so over the hill that he couldn't take this punk down. But how many others here shared Art's attitude about former cops asking questions? And he wasn't about to stand back out of sight and let Chelsea put herself in the middle of a crowd filled with attitudes like Kendrick's and men like Vaughn, who had a *unique relationship with reality.* Although he knew she would willingly volunteer to conduct the interviews, it was too dangerous.

And priority one—even more important than finding his son—was keeping Chelsea safe.

"Arthur." There was a reprimand in Tess's tone now. "Chelsea used to be one of us. I'll vouch for her. She wouldn't bring anyone here who wasn't safe."

While Art didn't seem thrilled with Buck being there, he seemed to respect Tess's authority. With a groan of protest, he held out his hand. "You got a picture of this guy you're looking for?"

Buck pulled out his phone but didn't immediately hand it over. "I didn't say it was a guy."

Art shrugged. "I assumed. It'd probably be easier for Gerald to see a picture and tell you yes or no that he's seen him than to try to get any reliable details out of him."

Buck showed him Bobby's picture. "Have you seen this young man?"

Although he stared at the image long enough, Art didn't answer Buck's question. Instead, he turned to Tess and excused himself. "I'd better make sure the kitchen is ready. Friday is always a full night. With that old dishwasher out of commission, we'll be slammed in the kitchen."

Before Buck realized her intent, Chelsea reached out and grabbed Art by the rolled-up sleeve of his blue work shirt. "Do you know Bobby?" she asked, insisting the other man answer. "You were fascinated by the picture. He looked familiar to you. If you don't want to talk to Buck, talk to me."

"No." Buck was pulling Chelsea away from the former gangbanger at the same time Art plucked her fingers from his sleeve. "You talk to *me*."

Art shook his head as he backed out the door. "I don't have time to talk to anyone. The front desk will let you know when Gerald arrives. I need to make sure my kitchen is ready for service."

"Rude." Chelsea turned and tilted her gaze up to Buck. "Did you see the look in his eyes? It was like he was taking a trip down memory lane. Could he have gone to school with Bobby? Maybe he remembers something from back then. Maybe he was one of the bullies who harassed him, and he's feeling bad about what he did."

"Maybe he thinks your boy is cute." Tess had moved in behind Chelsea, essentially blocking the door.

"Why would you say that?" Chelsea spun to face her friend again. "Is Art gay? Not that all LGBTQ+ people know each other, but it looked to me like he might have recognized Bobby."

"Don't you go pestering him tonight. I need him." Tess fluttered her hands, waving aside Chelsea's speculation. "Whatever you think you saw in Art might just be his temper brewing."

Beyond Tess's shoulder, Buck saw Art stop at the front desk, probably to deliver the message about Gerald. But then the young man's dark eyes briefly met Buck's before he dashed into the dining area.

Nope. Buck's threat radar was still pinging all over the place. There was something up with that young man.

Could Art and Bobby have had an encounter of some

kind? Did he think the fact that Bobby was missing, and a retired cop was looking for him make him worry about being a suspect in Bobby's disappearance? Did he know something about the crimes where Bobby's DNA had been found? Buck wanted five minutes alone with Arthur Kendrick to find out what the man was hiding.

"Excuse his manners," Tess went on. Buck had to wonder if she was consciously stalling for time to let her cook retreat to the kitchen. "Arthur is an honest-to-goodness chef. He got tired of the long hours and extra pressure of running a restaurant kitchen. We've been eating like royalty around here lately. Even on our budget. I'm lucky to have him on staff. It's good to have a couple of extra men living on the premises full-time, too. The cops are good about answering our calls if we really need them. But it makes things feel safer. I'm not as young as I used to be, you know."

A couple of extra men? Buck didn't miss the slip. Was there a potential witness on the premises—someone besides Art and Gerald—who might know something about Bobby? "Is it possible to get a list of your staff—full and part-timers—and regular residents? I'm not with KCPD anymore, so I can't compel them to talk to me. But if they're willing, I'd like to ask them a few questions."

"As long as it's their choice. I'll email the staff names and contact information to Chelsea." The older woman's shoulders lifted with an apology. "Our resident list is confidential. But since you're joining us for dinner, you're welcome to see if anyone here is willing to talk to you."

"Thanks."

"Come on, we'd better get to work." Tess linked her arm through Chelsea's and pulled her into step beside her. Buck shut the door behind him, still unable to shake the feeling that he was missing something here. Either the homeless shelter was hiding something about his son—or there were other secrets here that Tess and Art, or maybe someone else, weren't eager for him to discover.

Chapter Twelve

"Stop. How long have those pans been sitting in the water?"

Art Kendrick shot off another text before nudging Chelsea aside. He set his cell phone on the shelf above the industrial sinks where she'd been washing dishes for the past hour and thrust his tattoos into the sudsy water up to his elbows.

"I just put them in," she protested, pointing to the laminated chart above the sink where the chef's explicit instructions on the care and handling of his pans and knives was clearly posted. "Hot water. No soaking. No scrubbing."

He wiped the clean skillet with the soft dishcloth, as she had. He plucked up the steel wool ball floating in the water and tossed it into the trash can at the end of the drain board. "I don't want that metal scrubber anywhere near my pots and pans."

"I didn't use—"

"I've got 'em seasoned the way I like them, and that'll ruin the finish."

Chelsea could have argued that she'd already washed another pan the way he was demonstrating and had used the steel wool on the bottom of a sheet tray that had gotten charred in the oven. But she let the needless demonstration continue and focused on the unattended phone, which had been Art's constant companion since she'd taken over dishwashing duty and Buck had been sent out into the dining area to bus tables. In between stirring the vat of pasta sauce on top of the stove, whirring up compound butter in the food processor and serving the shelter's clients, Art had been texting back and forth in an almost frantic conversation. Though whether the intensity of his reaction to the texts was because of the messages themselves or because their frequency interrupted his tyrannical rule over the Yankee Hill Shelter kitchen, she couldn't tell.

Yet.

But if she could separate him from his cell long enough, she'd be able to look at it and see whom he was texting. It would be an easy hack since she'd caught him typing in the four-digit unlock code when she was at the serving window beside him, dishing up chicken parmesan and spaghetti. He'd set his cell down then, too, but had quickly snatched it up the moment she pointed out that he had an incoming text from someone simply labeled C. He'd immediately sent her to the back of the kitchen for scullery detail, making her suspect that whomever he was texting—or whatever he was texting about—had something to do with her or Buck or the questions they'd been asking.

The fact that he'd sent Buck out front and was keeping his distance from him only solidified her suspicion that the man was hiding something he didn't want Buck to know. But did Art's abrasive behavior have anything to do with Bobby's disappearance? Maybe the bun-sporting chef had a secret of his own he wanted to keep from the former cop—a drug habit, an arrest warrant, his immigration status. Maybe he was the man who had attacked Gerald Vaughn in the alley outside, and who had somehow manipulated the DNA to throw suspicion off himself. Although, the simple 1-2-3-4 unlock code on his phone made her question how tech-savvy Art might be. Maybe the C he kept texting was the one with the hacking abilities.

Whatever was going on, Chelsea intended to find out. Computers were her thing, and a cell phone was a tiny computer, right? Buck might be the one asking questions and showing Bobby's picture, but she was his partner on this investigation—and she fully intended to do whatever she could to help him find the answers he needed.

"Get a clean towel," Art ordered, setting the pan in the drainer. "I don't want this air-drying. If it rusts, you'll owe me a new pan."

"Do you talk down to all your volunteers this way? No wonder Tess has trouble finding help. Scoot over." Chelsea nudged him right back out of her way, partly because she was tired of his rudeness, but mostly because she wanted him to move on to his next task and forget about his cell phone for a few minutes so she could steal a look at it. She'd lost track of all the people Buck had talked to out front, and though she didn't mind helping with this menial task, she wanted to be doing something to help move their search for Bobby forward, too. After a scuffle with one of the clients who'd come in high and looking for trouble, Buck had insisted she stay tucked away behind the scenes in the kitchen, where the only harm that could come to her was the virtual, irritating rash that Chef Kendrick's micromanaging was giving her.

"Art!" One of his assistants shouted across the kitchen. "My pies exploded and are overflowing into the bottom of the oven. It's making a mess."

"Did you cut slits in the top to vent them?"

"What?"

Art cursed. "Pull them out. Now," he ordered, already drying his hands and backing toward the oven. He tossed the damp towel at Chelsea. "Think you can get it right this time?"

Forcing a smile onto her face hurt. "I'll try."

The moment Art was back in the cooking area, salvaging fruit pies and ordering his assistant to grab a box of aluminum foil, Chelsea peeled off the rubber gloves she wore and snatched his phone off the shelf. Keeping her back to Art and an eye over her shoulder, she quickly opened the phone and typed in 1-2-3-4.

The first thing she did was check C's number and tap it into her own phone. Then she scrolled through more than two dozen texts that were time-stamped almost immediately after their meeting in Tess's office.

Stay away tonight, Art's first text warned.

On my way back from the store now. What's up?

Judgment Day.

Chelsea glanced back to make sure Art was fully occupied with stemming the burnt pies and sticky oven crisis. *Judgment Day* must be a prearranged code. There was a gap of several minutes before C's next incoming text.

I'll set the groceries on the back stoop. I'll come back later.

No! Don't risk it. There are two of them asking questions. If they find out what we've done they could arrest us.

The police haven't found me yet. The FBI doesn't know I exist. You had nothing to do with my crimes. You'll be safe.

Police? FBI? Who was C, and what had he done?

Chelsea skimmed past the row of warning emoticons that reminded her too much of *Trouble*'s threats and read Art's reply.

BLACKMAIL. Remember?

Blackmail. Not the crime she and Buck were investigating. Assault. Murder. Nothing in any of the slew of DNA matches she'd found had anything to do with an extortion investigation. Chelsea's shoulders sagged in frustration. She'd reached another dead end. It seemed like Art and this C were involved in something illegal. But whether or not it had anything to do with Bobby, she couldn't tell.

She skimmed through photos of a spoiled pit bull receiving multiple tummy rubs, the back of a blond-haired man walking the muscular dog, and what had apparently been a colorful autumn hiking excursion through Swope Park. A pan clattered to the floor, and glass shattered behind her. As she jumped at the loud noise, the phone flew from her fingers. She managed to knock it onto the drainboard before it landed in the dishwater, but she had to scramble after it to return to the home screen before Art declared he'd had enough incompetence in his kitchen. Chelsea hugged the phone to her stomach as she looked over her shoulder to see one of the volunteers stooping over a sheet pan and two pie plates with the contents sloshed across the floor. Tess hurried over to ease the tension between the two men and help clean up the accident. Was Art Kendrick always this high-strung and temperamental? Or had her and Buck's visit, and whatever he was helping his friend C cover up, triggered his nerves?

Deciding she didn't want that temper turned on her again, Chelsea lifted Art's phone to replace it on the shelf. But before she let go, a new text popped up on the screen.

It was from C.

How does he look?

Chelsea's heart rate charged into overtime. Why would C text that? She stretched up on tiptoe to spot Buck in the dining room and saw him shaking hands with an elderly Black man before pushing a slice of pie across the table to him. Did C know Buck? Who else could he be referring to? He was the only one here asking questions. Art had warned C to stay away, that the cops were at the shelter. Who else would care about how Buck looked except for his son? Chelsea's pulse raced with anticipation until—

"What the hell are you doing? Nosy much?" She barely swiped her way back to the home screen before Art twisted her arm and grabbed his phone from her grasp.

Cringing at the pain radiating through her wrist, Chelsea answered with the first lie she could think of. "I knocked it off the shelf. I was trying to save it from a watery grave. I turned it on to see if it still worked."

Art tightened the fingers clamped around her arm. "Are you reading my texts?"

"Get your hand off her, Kendrick."

Chelsea felt the heat of Buck's body at her back a split second before she jumped at the bang of the tray of dirty dishes he dropped onto the counter beside her.

Art swore at the crashing sound and released her. He waved his phone at Buck. "Don't you need a search warrant for this kind of invasion of privacy?" he challenged.

"I'm not a cop," Buck reminded him. Although, moving his shoulder between Chelsea and Art, and forcing the younger man to back up a step, he indicated his protective instincts hadn't gotten one bit rusty since leaving KCPD. "I am the guy who's going to stop you from manhandling this woman."

Art glared at Chelsea, then tipped his chin at the larger man. His nostrils flared with agitated breaths. "No one here is giving up their friends. Maybe your son doesn't want to be found."

He strode away, disappearing out the back door of the kitchen into the alleyway before Chelsea's vision filled with the breadth of Buck's chest.

"Are you hurt?" Buck slid his calloused hand along her jaw, while Chelsea's hands fisted into his shirt at either side of his waist.

"I *was* reading his texts," Chelsea confessed, although her mind was replaying Art's words. "He's been talking to someone named C ever since we got here, warning him to stay away from the shelter. And then C asked about *you*. At least, I think he was talking about you. Like he knows you personally. And there was something about blackmail. But I don't know if he's doing the blackmailing, or he intends to blackmail you, or—"

"Are. You. Hurt?" Two hands framed her jaw now, tilting her face up to Buck's.

Chelsea eased the protective anger brewing in his eyes with a quick shake of her head. She wrapped her fingers around his solid forearms and offered up a wry smile. "Rambling?"

The corner of his mouth crooked with one of those almost grins. "Spewing out thoughts right and left so fast I can't quite keep up." Something about her expression must have changed because his lips crept closer to an actual smile. "And the thoughts keep coming. What just went through that brain of yours?"

"'Friends'?" Art's declaration felt like something more than the clichéd code of the street. "Art said no one around here would give up their *friends*. Do you think he's friends with Bobby?"

Buck's shoulders lifted with a massive shrug, and he shifted his grip to cradle the wrist Art had grabbed between both of his. "He's not anyone I ever knew Bobby to hang out with. Four years is a long time for him to be off living his own life, though. No one around here seems to know anyone named Bobby or Buckner. The ones who'll talk to me, anyway." He strummed his thumb across the handprint on her skin. "That's going to leave a bruise. I'd like to leave a mark on Kendrick, teach him some manners. What set him off?"

Although Chelsea was completely aware of the warmth of Buck's hands on her skin, and the tingling frissons each stroke of his thumb was infusing into her pulse, her brain was focused on piecing together the disparate pieces of the puzzle she'd been working on for months. "He's awake and breathing. That's enough for Art to be upset, I think." Buck chuckled, but she could tell he wasn't going to let the question drop. "He's hiding something. Protecting someone. I was pushing to find out what. When he wouldn't talk to me, I helped myself to a few answers. That made him a little testy."

"He doesn't get to touch you like that." Alarm flattened his mouth back into its familiar grim line. "You don't think he's *Trouble*, do you?"

"I'm okay, Buck." She paused to cup his stubbled jaw, the same way he'd just held her. "And no, I don't." Then she tugged on her rubber gloves and resumed her dishwashing duties. "What did you find out from Gerald?"

"My high school English teacher could use him as a case study in metaphors." Buck worked beside her, separating trash from the dishes before setting them in the soapy water. "He answered everything as though we were talking about a football game. He described his assault like a football play. He was the quarterback, and the defensive line charged him—I'm guessing maybe some gang members were harassing him? When I showed him Bobby's picture, he talked about the linebacker breaking through the line to get to the quarterback. Although, it was hard to tell whether the man he described was one of his attackers, or someone protecting him."

Chelsea set the last of the pans on the drainboard, putting Buck on drying detail, and started in on the last of the dishes. "Art looks more like a gang member than Bobby."

"Although he's added plenty of other ink, he's got Westside Warrior tats on him."

"Art was in a gang?"

Buck nodded. "Tess or someone else must have rescued him. Or he wouldn't be working here."

"A lot of rescues seem to happen in this part of town, don't they?" She tilted her gaze up to his. "Not everybody has a good guy in their corner like I do."

She felt Buck's fingers sifting beneath her ponytail to clasp the nape of her neck. He pressed his lips to her forehead, where they lingered long enough to make her shiver with want. "I will always be here for you, Chels."

She leaned into his strength, feeling cherished, protected. But did he love her? Could he possibly? Was she projecting her own feelings for him and turning friendship, chemistry and a bone-deep sense of duty into something more? Why couldn't she figure out this relationship between them?

Why couldn't she find Bobby? Why couldn't she figure out *Trouble*'s threats and the incursions into the cases she'd been researching for the crime lab?

Friends. Linebackers. Rescue. C. *Trouble*. Bullets. Motorcycle. Art Kendrick. Dennis Hunt. Bobby Buckner. Bikers. Sin City. Threats against her pets. False DNA matches. *Stay in your corner of the web, bitch.*

The answers were there, taunting her like a missing piece of code that would make the program running inside her head finally make sense if she could just find the connection that allowed everything to fall into place. "What else did you learn?" she asked, turning back to the sink.

The data swirled through Chelsea's thoughts as Buck continued. "I talked to a young woman named Brandy Tolliver. She's taking business classes at the community college. She was on her laptop, doing homework. She told me it was either buy the computer or pay her rent. She's helping Tess with some accounting in exchange for room and board until she can get on her feet again."

"I know Brandy. She made some bad choices a few years back, but she's a good person. Did she tell you anything useful?"

"She said Bobby's picture reminded her of a guy who works at the shelter. Lives upstairs and offers a little extra security. The guy met her at the bus stop at night and walked her to the shelter more than once."

"Brandy thinks this protector is Bobby? But she didn't recognize his name?"

Buck shrugged. "She wouldn't say for sure. Wish I had a more recent picture. The guy she knows is big and muscular. A lot blonder than Bobby."

"Big and muscular—like a linebacker?"

"I guess."

"Is it possible that this protector is the same man Gerald was trying to tell you about?" That missing piece of code was starting to fit into place. "He wasn't hurting Gerald—he was helping him? Maybe fighting off his attackers?"

Buck considered the connection she was trying to

make. "There could have been blood from the fight that ended up on Gerald's box."

"The sample that popped as Bobby's DNA." Chelsea slipped the last plate into the drainer basket. "Brandy's protector was blond? Did she mention if the blond man had a pit bull?"

"No."

"Does this neighborhood security guard have a name? Could I look him up?" she asked.

"Clark Remington."

Clark.

C.

That piece of code dropped into place.

Chelsea dripped water over her shoes and the leg of Buck's jeans as she spun toward him. "Are you done interviewing clients out there? I need to get home to my computer."

"Chels." He gently took her wrists and guided her hands back over the sink. "Other than doing our civic duty, I think tonight is a bust."

"No." She vibrated with the need to get to a keyboard. She unplugged the drain and peeled off the gloves. She brushed her warm fingertips across the frown line above his eyebrow. "Intense. You're too close to this, Buck. This is what you came to me for all those months ago. I know what to do now." She beamed a smile up at him, willing him to share in her excitement. "Computers don't care. As long as you ask the right questions, they don't care what mood you're in. You can find the answers you need."

"What answers do you think you'll find? What do you know that I don't?"

"Drive me home now." Chelsea draped the gloves over the edge of the sink. "I need to do a little hacking."

"The kind where you lose yourself on the dark web, stay up all night and forget to keep an eye out for low-lifes like Hunt and *Trouble*?"

That sobering reminder tempered her enthusiasm. "Uh… Yes?"

Buck tucked a wayward lock of hair behind her ear. "You got a couch?"

She nodded.

"Then you hack away. Because I'll be staying the night, watching your back while you work." He leaned in and pressed his lips briefly against hers. Then his fingers tunneled into the base of her ponytail, cupping the nape of her neck and pulling her onto her toes before he covered her mouth with his again. His tongue teased the seam of her lips, and she eagerly parted them, welcoming the deep stamp of his mouth against hers. She braced her hands against his chest, swaying as he lifted his head and released her far too soon. "Put away whatever you need to here. I'll get our things from Tess's office."

"You kissed me."

"You okay with that?"

She licked her lips, savoring the heat still tingling there. "It wasn't a forehead kiss."

"No, it wasn't." Buck crowded into her personal space until she could feel the heat of his body from her breasts to her toes. "I have a thing for nerds who get excited about diving into data streams and doing research."

"You do?"

He touched the nosepiece of her glasses and nudged

them back into place. "For one nerd, in particular, I do," he admitted. He feathered his fingers into her hair again. "When your brain kicks into gear like this, it's a thing of beauty. But it leaves you vulnerable. It's my job to protect that—so you can shine, sweetheart. So you can do what you do and get the job done."

It wasn't a declaration of love, but he'd shown her in a dozen different ways already that he cared about her. Chelsea clung to the heat of Buck's promise. His faith in her abilities strengthened her. The mix of restrained passion and raw tenderness made her want to give everything she had to this man. "That may be the sweetest thing anyone has ever said to me. And, you can kiss me like that anytime."

"I'll keep that in mind." He released her entirely and stepped back. His shoulders lifted with a deep breath. Even without his holster and guns, he was putting on his protective armor again. "You never answered— what do you think you'll find?"

She didn't want to get Buck's hopes up if she was wrong, but she felt as if she was on the verge of solving at least one mystery. "C. I'm going to find C."

"What's C?"

"Not what. Who. Art's friend. Maybe his boyfriend since I think they live together. It's possible Art's C and Brandy's protector are one and the same. Maybe even the same guy as Gerald's linebacker."

"You're not making sense."

She needed concrete evidence to prove what her hopeful instincts were screaming at her. Her old-school alpha male hero would settle for nothing less. "I need to follow the digital breadcrumbs."

"Who is C, Chels?"

"Clark Remington. I need to find him. I think he might have the answers we're looking for."

"All right. I'll trust that means something important." Buck scanned the kitchen to make sure Art was still outside where he couldn't get to Chelsea. "Kendrick comes back in, you yell for me, okay? He doesn't get to be rude to you or touch you, understand?"

Chelsea smiled. "Okay."

She watched Buck stride out into the lobby. Eleven months of painstaking research were about to pay off. Chelsea crossed her fingers down at her sides. Once she had proof that her suspicions were correct, the man she loved would finally, truly, fully smile. He might even feel like he could love again—that he could love her. That he could live a full life that was about more than finding his son and keeping people safe.

"Clark's a protector…" she whispered "…like his father."

Chapter Thirteen

Chelsea sipped on her tepid green tea and watched the information loading onto her screen, willing her weary eyes and wired brain to focus.

Buck had called in several favors, so that there'd be someone watching her house around the clock. Chelsea's fur babies were safe, and her home was secure. Despite the presence of dogs on the property and someone from KCPD, the lab or Buck's security firm parked outside, Buck still gave the house one more sweep before stepping into the shower. Then he'd thrown on a pair of sweats and stretched out on the blanket and pillows she'd set up on the living room couch.

Yes, she felt safer with Buck on the premises. But her brain seemed to be on the fritz, short-circuiting with the discovery that even in winter Buck slept without a shirt on, leaving nothing about those sturdy biceps and broad chest to her imagination. She learned that the sprinkling of silver among the brown curls dusting his chest narrowed into a straight line over the flat plane of his stomach and was just as sexy as the stubble shading his jaw. She'd offered him the bed in her spare bedroom, but since that was where she had her computers set up and would be working, he'd opted for the living room. Besides, he'd said he wanted to be between her and anything that might come in through that front door.

And while she'd rambled on about the state of his back come morning, Buck had kissed her lightly on the lips, stalling her arguments. By the time the desire his touch triggered inside her pushed its way past her startled confusion, and she was stretching up to deepen the kiss, Buck had pulled away with a ragged breath. He pressed another kiss to her forehead, warned her not to stay up too late, and promised he'd be sleeping with one eye open to make sure she got to bed safely.

Her brain fritzed again when she stepped into the bathroom to take care of her own business. The small room overwhelmed her with its lingering heat and scents that were piney and clean and overtly masculine. Had she ever smelled anything so delicious as the mix of Buck's shower gel and the man himself? She could easily imagine the heat coming off his body after the steamy shower and nuzzling her nose into the arousing scents that clung to his skin.

Chelsea had changed into her own pajamas and slipper socks and snugged herself inside a hoodie before discovering that Rafael and Donatello had switched their loyalties and snuggled up on the couch with Buck. With Peanut Butter claiming her bed all for himself, there was only Jelly to keep her company as Chelsea fired up her computers and went to work. While the tuxedo cat lounged in the dog bed under Chelsea's desk and randomly hissed as though she was unhappy with all the lamps and computer screens being on in the room where she wanted to nap, Chelsea denied herself the creepy urges to either watch Buck sleep or lock herself in the bathroom to surround herself with his scent until the last bit of steam had dissipated.

Having Buck make himself at home in her space was at once calming and unsettling. And while every instinct in her wanted to go out to that couch and curl up against his heat and strength, she knew time was of the essence, and the answers they needed were almost within her reach.

Her brain finally began to cooperate once she heard Buck's measured breathing from the living room, and she got swept up in her research. Jelly quieted and Chelsea disappeared into the tunnel of the dark web and got lost in her work.

Information on Clark Remington was sparse, but relatively easy to find. It hadn't taken much to gain access to Tess Washington's records at the shelter. He was the only Clark she'd found from the past four years. He was a former resident who had gone on to be part of the shelter's payroll. He'd been scheduled to work tonight but had never logged in on the employee computer, thanks to Art's texts warning him away, no doubt. With a phone number and an employment history to work with, she'd done a deep dive and discovered that Clark hadn't existed until four years ago, matching the timeline of Bobby's disappearance. Fake IDs and new identities were usually the purview of criminals and Witness Protection. Even with her skills, however, WITSEC was a hard system to crack. So she'd leaned hard into a few less reputable sites and found the image of a driver's license for a C. Remington. It looked like some enterprising individual had created an online site where, for a modest price, college students and high schoolers could buy fake IDs to make themselves seem older, and anyone who wanted to stay off the grid could be transformed into a whole new person.

The aptly named *Identity Eraser* website was now defunct, but since nothing ever completely disappeared from the web, Chelsea was able to glean through the information someone had tried to dismantle and bury. C. Remington had paid a hundred bucks for the fake ID, but she'd found no photographs for Clark beyond the blurry image on the license. He was blond and buff, like the man in Art Kendrick's pictures, and as Brandy Tolliver had described the shelter's resident protector. Maturity, working out and hair dye could explain the changes between Bobby Buckner's high school photo and Clark Remington. But with shaggy hair and glasses distorting his face, Chelsea was unable to confirm that she'd found the older version of Buck's missing son.

Beyond comparing DNA samples to prove that she'd found Bobby—which seemed pretty ironic given the circumstances—she needed to see the man. Talk with him. She needed to take her own picture and make the comparison. She scoured social media sites and found no Clark Remington who even vaguely matched the blurry image. She even studied Art Kendrick's posts, but there were more pictures of the dog than of the blond man—and none that showed his face.

That meant meeting with this stranger in person, which she doubted Buck would allow without him being present—but she didn't want to raise any false hopes before she could confirm Clark's identity. Could she lure him somewhere so she could get a look at him on a camera feed? She doubted she could convince Clark to come to the crime lab or one of the KCPD precinct stations, and Art would keep him out of sight at the shelter for the time being. But what if she could talk Clark into meeting her someplace else where she had easy access to say, a security camera? With the solution percolating in her head, she picked up her phone and typed in a lengthy text to Clark.

Hey, Clark. My name is Chelsea O'Brien. Sorry to text so late. (Bad habit of mine.) I'm hoping UR asleep and won't read this til morning. I'm a good friend of Robert Buckner's. UR a hard man to find. But if UR who I think, we need to talk. I saw your message to Art K., asking about Buck.

She fudged the next part of her message—it wasn't exactly a lie, given Buck's guilt and heartbreak, but it could be interpreted as a reference to some risky health issue. He's not good. I know you dropped out of his life for what I'm sure is a good reason. But he really needs to see you. Could we talk? Please call or txt this number. He doesn't know I'm contacting you. Depending on your response, he never has to know. But please, hear me out. If it helps to know, he retired from KCPD to devote more time and resources to finding you. (That's where I come in. I'm good at finding things. Did you know you're still listed on the IDENTITY ERASER website?) Also…someone is trying to frame you for several crimes, including murder. My money is on you being innocent because of other suspicious stuff I've uncovered. BTW, if you really want to disappear off the web, I can help with that. I won't charge anything except a conversation with you.

Please contact me.

If it really was Bobby, she had a feeling she'd get a response—at least a cautious one asking for more information, or maybe a pithy reply telling her exactly what she could do with her invasive request. If he wasn't Bobby, then Clark would dismiss her as a crazy lady and simply delete her message.

"Please be Bobby," she prayed, plugging her phone into its charger and clicking off her link to the *Identity Eraser* website.

She might have gone to bed then, but her probe into the *Identity Eraser* site must have pinged an alert with whoever had created the old site, and she sat up straight. The information link that had been inactive moments ago now highlighted as her cursor cruised over it. The next thing she knew, she was being taken to a new screen. "Oh, hell."

Rookie, brain-fritzing, distracted hacker mistake.

Someone was active on the other end of her probe. The website graphics disappeared from her screen, just as the screen grabs from Vinnie's security camera had. The driver's license transaction disappeared, and another image popped up on her screen. A familiar image.

It was Chelsea herself. The same grainy photo she'd found tucked against her windshield seconds before the shooting at Sin City. A picture from someone who'd watched her outside the bar. Her breath stuttered in her chest as bright red letters marched across the screen. This was no warning about staying in her own corner of the web. No threat that someone would get hurt if she didn't stop hacking her way to the truth.

There was just one word.

Erased.

"Trouble."

Even as the threat burned into her retinas, Chelsea pushed aside her tea and went on the offensive. This guy was online right now. That meant she could digitally track him. She could follow his trail straight through to whatever corner of the internet where he was hiding. He knew she had discovered his illegal transactions, and he was trying to cover his tracks.

A defunct website layered over an active one was a pretty good way to hide secrets from most people surfing the web. But Chelsea wasn't most people. Not when it came to her tech. Her pulse hammered in her ears as she broke into the site and deleted the disturbing graphic. Before she could get into the source code and home in on his location, he sent a slew of pornographic pop-up ads to her screen. It took her a minute, but she got off the ads and back to the screen that led her one step closer to finding *Trouble*. Like any artist who had his or her own unique style, most hackers tended to write code in a familiar style that could be traced if someone knew what to look for.

Chelsea knew.

Their online duel of incursions and blocks continued for several minutes before Chelsea gained the upper hand.

"Gotcha!" A new set of images with links and graphics loaded onto her screen. She'd tapped into a whole new version of the *Identity Eraser* site.

Murder Eraser.

She read the brief graphic at the top of the screen. *Commit a crime? I can make any charges against you go away. Contact me for a price quote.*

The entrepreneur who'd made a few extra bucks off Clark Remington and others had graduated into an enterprise that was equally illegal, but much more dangerous. He was still in the identity changing business. But now, instead of simply altering the customer's name or date of birth on a piece of plastic, he was altering their very DNA. Well, not altering the actual DNA… "Mislabeling it," she breathed out loud.

In a way, *Trouble*'s scheme wasn't much more complicated than his original scam had been. Only, instead of saying Bobby Buckner's picture was now Clark Remington, for example—he was saying that an unknown sample of DNA was now Bobby's. Or it belonged to some other poor schlub who'd had the misfortune to do business with *Trouble*. That was why her new DNA matches kept going back to the same pool of names—*Trouble* was limited to using the IDs from his old website. Limited to using the old identities he'd been paid to change. Although creating a fake ID was a much lesser charge than tampering with a police investigation, it was still a crime. But was it enough of a crime that *Trouble* was *blackmailing* those clients into keeping their mouths shut about borrowing their old identities? Was that what Art had meant in his text to Clark? Or were they even aware they were being used in that way?

Chelsea locked onto a line of code and followed it into the guts of the *Murder Eraser* site. Simplistic and repetitive as the scam might be, there was a huge difference in the amount of money *Trouble* was making now.

"Oh my God." She lifted her fingers from the keyboard for a second as a spreadsheet popped up. Ten thousand dollars. Five thousand dollars. A hundred grand? "Buck?" she whispered out loud, knowing he needed to see this.

What was she looking at here? A business ledger? A banking record? Payments? Receipts? For what? One column held initials. Then contact information—emails or phone numbers. Another the monetary amount. A fourth looked like purchase orders. No, they were case numbers.

Chelsea squinted to bring the information into focus and decipher its meaning. KCPD case numbers? Court dockets?

She recognized one case number as the Lukinburg Embassy John Doe murder since she'd spent so much time poring over the file. It was next to the hundred-grand listing. The initials on a different line were WW. She doubted this guy would be paying out or receiving $1,000 for a weight loss program. *Westside Warriors?* Art Kendrick's former gang? They were a known entity in the No-Man's Land area of downtown Kansas City. She read *MTMC* on another line. Surely, those initials didn't stand for Missouri Twisters Motorcycle Club. While Gordy and his bros would certainly show up on police reports, they were into engines and machinery, not digital footprints and databases. She had eighteen tainted cases at the crime lab. There were eighteen entries on this list—with three more cases listed, but no money recorded. "Those clients haven't paid. You haven't done the job yet."

And if a client didn't or couldn't pay—*Trouble* had the perfect setup to blackmail them by linking their real identity to the case they were involved in. She quickly scanned the initials again, looking for a BB or a CR. Maybe planting Bobby's DNA at those crime scenes *was* the blackmail. Maybe that was what these numbers meant.

Knowing she needed a detective or forensic analyst from the lab to make sense of what she'd found, Chelsea took a couple of screen grabs of the spreadsheet and saved them onto a data stick and her cloud drive. This time, *Trouble* wasn't stealing back any evidence she'd found. And if she could find him, KCPD could make an arrest.

All she needed was an address. The location of the other hacker's user terminal. *Trouble*'s real name.

The feeling that she was on the verge of breaking through the final barrier and nailing this faceless SOB to the wall tingled through her fingertips and made her heart pound. A hacker for hire. The same shady sort of success she might have become if Mac Taylor hadn't seen her skills in action and hired her on the spot to work for the crime lab instead. The draw of becoming a valuable part of a team after she'd spent so much of her life alone, of helping others the way she'd needed to be helped, had convinced her to put on her white hat. To help take down criminals like *Trouble* and the man who'd shot at her and Buck and whoever had killed that poor man outside the Lukinburg Embassy.

Since the results of her hacking skills were rarely admissible in court, she'd need a warrant to document her findings. Tracking this guy wasn't good enough. Buck, KCPD and her friends at the crime lab all wanted to be able to make an arrest on this guy stick. She might have hit paydirt, but she'd need to run a case-by-case match to make sense of what she was looking at. Chelsea sat back for a moment as the tension locked up her neck and shoulders. It had been a long day and a longer night, on top of a long week. She was physically and mentally spent, but she wasn't done working yet.

"Stay in my own corner of the web…" she muttered, probing even deeper to find where *Trouble* was accessing the deep web right now. Definitely Kansas City. The first address she hit on was bogus, but she kept following the trail. Williams University. Was this guy a student? A bored young coed who was ruining lives for grins and giggles? A professor who needed money? She pulled off her glasses to give her weary eyes a break and turned to her laptop to make herself a note to run names of students and staff against anyone with computer expertise who owned a motorcycle and had experience firing a gun like the one used to terrorize her at Sin City.

Breathing quickly now, as if running a race, Chelsea turned back to her main screen to find the hacker she was after. Not the Computer Sciences building. Not even a computer lab. An office? A dorm room? He was definitely bouncing off a campus address. "I'm coming for you, *Trouble*. I will find you and stop you." Not on campus, but from a location close by. "Who…? Are…? You…?"

Perhaps picking up on her mistress's tension, Jelly meowed in a low, discordant tone that sounded as if she was in mortal pain from under the desk. "Shush, Jelly, you're all right. I need to concentrate."

Chelsea was a few keystrokes away from pinging the cybercriminal's home address when an alert popped up on the screen of her second computer. He was flooding her email account again. He couldn't stop her, so he was working around her, distracting her, fighting back in the only way he had left. But she'd ignore whatever junk he was sending to her inbox. He could send her all the threats he wanted. It would be more evidence to use against him once she identified him.

"Chels?" A deep, rumbly voice called to her from the doorway. "It's four in the morning, sweetheart. Have you been up this whole—?"

"Shh!" Typically, Buck's voice soothed her, aroused her. His appearance was probably what had set the cat off. She could feel Jelly puffing up and twisting around her legs. "Oh, I am all up in your corner of the web now." She was so close. She didn't need the distraction of Buck's drowsy, sexy voice getting under her skin and distracting her. Now wasn't the time for the rare cuddle from her persnickety cat, either. Chelsea was closing in on *Trouble*. In his neighborhood. On his server.

"Did you just shush me?" She was obliquely aware of Buck moving across the room. His hand settled on the back of her chair. "Where are your glasses? You're going to have one hell of a crick in your back all hunched over like that." His big, warm palm settled between her shoulder blades. A riot of goose bumps pricked the back of her neck as her tense muscles jumped at the sudden heat.

As good as that felt, she shrugged him off. "Don't touch me!"

He stepped away from her. Drowsy, sexy, soothing Buck was gone. "I see what you mean about being obsessive. How long have you…?"

"I've almost got him." She followed the digital breadcrumbs like a twisty path straight to her target.

"Got who? Are you messing with that creep—?"

"Yes!" She pumped her fist and sat back briefly before turning back to her laptop to record the location. But Jelly had had enough of lights and talking and surprises. She leaped up onto the desk to plop herself down right in front of Chelsea's face, lifting a paw to lick it. "Jelly!" she groused, pushing the cat aside before she rolled over onto her keyboards and accidentally added a command or deleted a link. When the cat had cleared her line of sight, Chelsea read the victory lighting up her screen. "Now who's the best!"

"Chels?" Buck picked Jelly up from the corner of the desk, hugged the cat briefly against his chest and set the furball down on the daybed behind them. He was back at her side, kneeling beside her chair, before Jelly's easy acceptance of Buck's presence and touch registered. Wait a minute. Had her standoffish cat allowed the caress she had rejected? Chelsea blinked and shook her head as if waking from a stupor. Why would she do that? Had she dreamed Buck being here? Where was his shirt? My God, she loved his big arms. Was she still lost in a cyberspace twilight zone? For a few seconds, Chelsea's thoughts splintered between work and desire, victory and regret.

She reached over to stroke her fingertips across the sandpapery stubble lining Buck's jaw. Up close and personal like this, she could see the tremor of his muscles responding to her touch. Definitely real. "Buck? I didn't mean to push you away. I was concentrating. I'm sorry. And yes, I should apologize this time," she added before he thought about lecturing her. "Are you mad at me?"

"I'm not mad. I'm worried about you." He mirrored

the same gesture, stroking his fingers across her jaw to study her face. "Have you slept at all?"

His gentle touch and assessing eyes gave her a boost of energy, and clarity returned. She pointed to the numbers and code on her computer screen.

"I found *Trouble*." While the identifying information blinked on the screen, Chelsea turned to her laptop to plug in the IP address to pull up real-world contact information.

"Why is it pinging like that?" Buck asked, hearing the assault of emails that she'd tuned out.

"He's sending me threats. Probably has an automated setup targeting my system to try to crash it."

"Damn it, Chels—"

"It won't work. I let him have access to my laptop. It keeps him out of my big boy here. They're on different servers. Even if this one goes down, I've got the information I need saved."

He read the growing number of unread messages. "Those are all threats?"

"I've got a name." The adrenaline that had been fueling her ebbed, and the haze of code and digital tricks flooding her brain began to recede. But she fought back the exhaustion to keep the answers coming. "Tyson Hawthorne, Jr. An investment analyst? Wealthy man. Wealthy neighborhood. Why would he be screwing with the crime lab's DNA matches? Is this some elaborate cover-up to mask a crime he committed? Do you think he killed Yuri Dubrovnik? I doubt he'd be caught dead in No-Man's Land. Well, he probably would be dead if he was there—"

"Focus, sweetheart." Buck's blessedly warm, large hand cupped the nape of her neck, shocking her body with a wave of lucid heat. This time, she was aware enough to be grateful for Buck's calming touch. Now that she had an ID, though, she could access tons of information. She squinted toward the screen and kept reading. "He's married. To wife number two. Divorced from some socialite. Has a son who goes to Williams University—on and off. Engineering and computer science. Not a very good student, apparently. He's on the six-year-plus plan." Here were the stats she was looking for. "*You* look like a much better candidate for this kind of data manipulation. Tyson Jude Hawthorne the *third*." She frowned, skimming more data. "Why does that name sound familiar?" She pulled up Tyson III's university ID. "I know this guy."

"Is he online right now?" Buck pulled his cell phone from the pocket of his sweats. "Does he know who you are? Where you are?" His fingers kneaded the cords of tension in her neck, and she moaned at the mix of pain and relief. "I'm going to text Grayson to find out if he sees anything going on outside."

"Grayson?" The lab's blood expert? "Why would you text him?"

"He's helping me watch the house tonight." He shot off the text before returning his hand to the back of her neck. "You need to talk to me. Do you know who *Trouble* is?"

Chelsea turned and looked into whiskey-brown eyes that were close enough to read without her glasses. Checked impatience. Worry. The desire to understand. The need to take action. "It's TJ. That whiny guy at Sin City hiding behind a hooker in the back corner of the bar."

Buck swore. "The hoodie kid? He was that close to you?"

She didn't know whether to feel angry or afraid. "He was there the whole time. Close enough to clone my phone or tap into my Wi-Fi hot spot and read what I was doing online. He had a computer pad. He didn't care about Desiree or any of the other women. They were a front. An excuse for him to be there. He was working back in that damn corner while I was on my laptop following my leads on Bobby."

Buck's hand never left her neck as he punched in a number on his phone. "Give me an address on this guy."

Chelsea's fingers shook as she scrolled through the information. "He's been right under my nose this whole time. I got too close with my research, so he tracked me down. That's how he got a picture of me at the bar. That's how he could get into the security feed and make the images from the shooting disappear so quickly. He wasn't slumming. He was following me."

"An address, sweetheart," he urged.

"He's online right now at his father's house. Near the Plaza." There was plenty of public record information on his parents, as well. "Hey, look. Mom and Dad and stepmom all belong to the Pioneer Gun Club. Maybe that's where he learned to shoot."

"Does he own a motorcycle?"

Chelsea pulled up the DMV records and nodded. "There's your hat trick. Computer expertise. Access to a gun. Motorcycle tag." Her eyes could barely focus. But it didn't matter, she'd found the truth. "Those threats had nothing to do with Dennis's trial. TJ didn't want me to find his *Murder Eraser* site."

"*Murder Eraser?* I hate the sound of that."

"For the right price, he'll hack into different databases and relabel your DNA, basically erasing you from a crime scene. Making you invisible to the crime lab."

"While throwing some innocent like Bobby onto the prime suspect list."

"Yeah. About that—"

"Rufe." Buck pushed to his feet as his call picked up, leaving his thumb to trace comforting circles at the back of her neck. "Sorry to wake you, my friend. I need a squad car to pick up our hacker who's been screwing with the crime lab's database."

"She found him?" When she heard Sergeant King's groggy reply, she realized Buck had the call on speakerphone. Chelsea heard him mumble something to his wife about going back to sleep. "The scumbag who's been terrorizing Chelsea?"

"Yeah. TJ Hawthorne."

"Give me the numbers. I'll pick him up myself."

"Thanks, Rufe. I owe you one."

"Don't you dare thank me. I want this lowlife to stop messin' with my crime lab and my friends as much as you do. Chelsea there?"

"I'm here, Rufus."

"Good work, girlfriend. You've earned your weekend off. Now you let me do my job, and let the old man take care of you, okay?"

"Thanks. I will." She glanced up at Buck's blurry face, unable to read his expression. "If he wants to." After the call was disconnected, she turned her chair toward Buck. "I'm sorry. I didn't mean to push you away. That felt good when you rubbed my back. I love it when you touch me. I wasn't thinking."

"You didn't have a Dennis moment where I freaked you out?"

"Is that what you thought?" As if Buck could ever remind her of her attacker. "No. I was having a Chelsea moment where all I could see was the code in front of me." She shrugged an apology and winced at the pain radiating through her shoulders. She picked up her glasses and faced her computer again. "I have to fix this mess. I can't let *Trouble*—er, TJ—taint any more of our cases and destroy the hard work everyone at the lab has done."

"None of this is on you." Buck knelt beside her again and plucked loose a tendril from beneath the earpiece of her glasses and tucked it behind her ear.

She shook her head. "Now that I know what I'm looking for, I can go in and correct all the misinformation. We'll still have unsolved cases, but there won't be any false leads or statistical errors defense attorneys can use against us. Once he's arrested, a judge can ban him from being online again. At least until after his trial. I need to contact Lexi about getting a search order for TJ's computers to get the ball rolling."

"You're not doing that tonight."

She opened her mouth again to tell him that her deep dive into *Trouble*'s illegal websites had also given her a lead on Bobby. "I need to follow up—"

But Buck's blunt finger pressed against her lips, silencing her. "You're running on fumes. Close down shop and get a couple hours of sleep. KCPD will have Hawthorne locked in an interview room and you can go back to working your behind-the-scenes miracles with fresh eyes in the morning." He nodded to her laptop. "And can you turn off that damn pinging sound?"

"It's annoying, isn't it?" Like the steady drip of a faucet. Like subliminal torture. Like the beat of the headache pounding against her skull. She turned her attention to the laptop. "Don't worry. I set up that account as a diversion so that I could move my personal information before he could access it. I'm saving them as evidence right now."

"But you can still read these messages?" She heard the frown in Buck's tone. "He's trying to intimidate you by loading up your workspace with his filth? No. Shut it down."

"All right, Bossy." She scrolled the mouse over to the Sign Out tab. She loved that Buck wanted to keep not just the physical danger, but the verbal assault, away from her. "You're adding harassment to the charges you're bringing against TJ, aren't you."

"Harassment. Cyberstalking. I'm sick and tired of men hurting you."

"No one's going to hurt me with Big Bad Buck Buckner—"

The moment she clicked the mouse, her screen exploded with pop-ups again.

Not any random pop-ups. Pictures of her.

Pictures of her right here. Right now.

Messy bun. Turquoise hoodie. Squinty, myopic eyes.

"What the hell?" Buck's curse matched her own.

"The camera." She immediately threw her hand over the tiny dot glowing above her computer screen. "He's hacked into my camera. Stupid rookie mistake."

"Shut it down!"

She switched off the camera, then raced through saving and shutting everything down. How long had he been watching her tonight? She'd been so focused on playing cat and mouse with *Trouble* that she hadn't realized that she was the mouse.

He was on the other side of the city, but she felt like she could hear *Trouble* laughing at her.

Before her screen went dark, another image appeared. Words this time. Even more unsettling than knowing he'd been watching her.

I will always be one step ahead of you and your cop friends.

Where's your black-and-white cat? I'd like to drop by and pet it. Maybe kill it after I take care of you and the dogs.

Hunt would pay me a fortune to make you go away.

But I'd do it for fun. To prove a point.

I'm. The. Best.

The words shattered into a thousand tiny pieces with the sound of a gunshot.

Chapter Fourteen

Chelsea jumped back at the sudden, concussive noise, screaming as her chair tipped and crashed to the floor. Buck was on top of her in an instant, shoving the chair aside and shielding her with his body. He reached beneath the desk and hit the power strip. The desk lamps all turned off, and her main computer dimmed as it switched to battery power.

"That son of a bitch." Buck dragged Chelsea partway beneath the desk, shielding her even further.

This felt eerily familiar. Her fingers dug into Buck's biceps. "No! Stay down."

Buck pushed himself up onto an elbow above her, keeping her flat on the floor with a hand on her shoulder while he surveyed the room around them. "It's okay. Not real bullets. It was on the computer."

"The ego on this guy. He can't beat me online, so he's going to kill the competition?"

Buck's big hand stroked her hair away from her face. "It's okay, sweetheart. No broken glass. No bullet holes. God, your heart's racing ninety miles a minute. Breathe with me, Chels. Open your eyes, sweetie, and look at me." She popped her eyes open and looked up into the mix of grim and tender in his face above hers. "I need you to slow your breathing. In. Out. Chels?"

"I can't… I can't do this anymore…" She couldn't even feel the weight of his body molded against hers. She couldn't stop shivering. "I thought it was real. I thought he was shooting at us again. Can someone literally be scared to death?"

"You're done," Buck said. He rolled to his feet and picked her up in his arms.

"I can find him again," she vowed. "I can fix this." Her cheek lolled against the juncture of his neck and shoulder, and she inhaled his heady, piney scent. But she couldn't seem to shake the code and hate and terror filling her thoughts. "I have to stop him, or he'll ruin every case we have."

There was a sharp knock at her back door, and she startled again. "Buck?" a man's voice shouted.

"He's here." Chelsea scrambled to escape and would have fallen to the floor if Buck hadn't tightened his arms around her.

"No more." He set her on the daybed behind her desk. Raphael and Donatello instantly sounded the alarm and ran through the house to meet their visitor. "Uh-uh, boys. This is Daddy's job." He scooped up a poodle in each hand and set them in her lap. "Keep Mama company." Once the dogs were secured in her arms, sharing all the heat and comfort twenty-four pounds of two small dogs could, Buck cupped either side of Chelsea's face and leaned in. "Rufus will get this Hawthorne kid. KCPD is on their way to his house right now." There was another knock and a shout for Buck. "That's Grayson. He's not a threat." He leaned in and pressed his lips to her forehead. "I'll be right back."

Chelsea's thoughts were still a hazy mess when she heard Grayson's voice at her back door. "Everything all right? I haven't seen anything since you texted me. But the hair on the back of my neck was standing up straight. Then the lights went out."

"I don't think it's a real-world threat. But he got to her online again," Buck answered. "She's crashing. Hard. Shock? Exhaustion? She needs to rest. I'll walk the perimeter myself, but will you stay the rest of the night and give me a heads-up if you see anything hinky going on?"

"Of course." She wondered how Grayson had gotten his wheelchair up the steps on her porch. He must be wearing his prostheses and crutches. "I don't know that I'm the best deterrent, though."

"You're a damn Marine. I trust you to have my back." The harshness of Buck's order eased with a deep breath. "Sorry, man. It kills me to see her like this. This guy is a cockroach. I don't think he's brave enough to take me on face-to-face. All I need is another set of eyes on the place—and that sixth sense that told you something was wrong—to watch things outside. I need to focus on taking care of Chelsea."

After a moment, Grayson agreed. "You got it. Give her a hug from me. If I feel like I'm jeopardizing her protection detail in any way, I'll call Jackson in to relieve me sooner. I don't like this guy playing with one of ours. It needs to stop."

"Agreed." She envisioned Buck shaking her coworker's hand. "Thanks, Malone."

After the lock reengaged, she saw the wounded warrior turned criminalist hobble past her office window in his awkward gait before relocking the door and sweeping the house. Then Buck threw on his boots and coat and grabbed his gun to go outside and secure the house.

Leaving everything as it was in her office, Chelsea roused herself enough to carry the dogs with her into her bedroom. By the time Buck was back inside, she'd curled up beneath the quilt with Donatello and Raphael tucked against her stomach on top of the covers. Peanut Butter snuggled in at her feet, and Jelly wasn't into giving any TLC.

Moments later, the mattress dipped behind her and Chelsea rolled downhill, feeling herself engulfed by more warmth than any number of pets could provide. Assured by Buck's scent, she didn't even open her eyes as he pulled her into his arms.

He removed her glasses and set them on the bedside table. "How bad is that headache?"

She squeezed her eyes open to find Buck's head on the pillow beside hers. "How do you know…?"

He pressed his thumb to the frown in the middle of her forehead. "You're squinting because the light hurts your eyes. And you didn't protest one whit when I got into bed with you."

"Why would I?" She folded her arms between them and snuggled into Buck's side, seeking his heat the way a moth sought the light. "I want you in bed with me." With her head on his shoulder and his arm curled behind her, he gently rubbed her neck, shoulders and back, easing the knots of tension there. "My couch wasn't comfortable enough?"

"It was too far away." His lips grazed her forehead. "Is this okay? You don't feel crowded or afraid with me here?"

"You're exactly where I need you to be." She pressed

her own lips to the swell of his pectoral muscle and felt the tremor of his response. "Nothing about the way you hold me reminds me in any way of Dennis Hunt or Randy Leighton. You're a man, not a bully. You're a living, breathing furnace, and my safe haven. I must have used up too many brain cells tonight. I'm so tired, Buck. So cold. God, I want you to make love to me. But I don't know how to make that happen."

She was rambling again, but Buck didn't seem to mind.

"It'll happen, sweetheart. But not tonight. You're on the brink of exhaustion from stress and lack of sleep and doing for everybody else but yourself." His arm tightened behind her back, pulling her closer. She suspected the movement of his hand had something to do with Raphael and Donatello and the sound of gently lapping tongues. "I want you awake and fully aware and an equal participant when I take you for the first time. Plus, I've got nothing against your pets, but I want only you and me in the bed when we make love."

The carnality of his words and his promise and his understanding of the weirdness that was her life seeped into her blood and warmed her from the inside out. "I love the sound of that. You want me, too?"

"Yeah, sweetheart. I want you. I'm done trying to do the right thing. I'm not even sure what the right thing is anymore. I was trying to keep either one of us from getting hurt. But all I'm feeling is lonely and frustrated and worried about you every damn minute you're out of my sight. I got you into this mess. And I will get you out of it. I hate seeing how this investigation is draining your beautiful spirit. I'm so sorry."

"I'm fine, Buck. My strength will come back." She

nuzzled the intoxicating scent of his skin. "In fact, I'm absorbing some of your strength right now."

"Take what you need," he offered. Chelsea nodded. She freed one arm from between them and wrapped it across his stomach. His hand rested on her forearm, securing her to him. "I love holding you like this. It calms something inside me. But know that I want you. Your body. That mouth. That perfect ass. Your smiles. Your brains. Your hope. I want all of you, Chels. I need all of you." His lips settled against her forehead with a familiar promise. "But you aren't ready for that tonight. Rest for now. We'll go back to saving the world in the morning."

"Would you kiss me?"

He rolled onto his side, facing her. And just as she thought he would kiss her forehead, which she would have been content with, he nestled a finger beneath her chin and tilted her face up to his.

And then his lips were on hers, exploring, consuming. Feeling one last jolt of energy charge through her system, she stretched up beside him to deepen the pressure, to push her tongue into his mouth. His fingers worked the bun loose atop her head and threaded into her hair. He clutched her scalp as he gently bit down onto the curve of her bottom lip, then soothed it with a raspy sweep of his tongue.

Moaning at the tingles of excitement making her lips sensitive to every lick, every nip, every caress, she skimmed her palms across his jaw. His hand reached down and squeezed her bottom as she slid her arms around his neck. She hugged, he pulled, and they rolled until Buck was lying on his back and Chelsea was on top of him. Her legs fell open across his hips. Even through the layers of sweatshirt and cotton, the tips of her breasts pearled and begged for the friction of his hard chest beneath hers. He slipped his hand beneath the waistband of her pajamas, branding her with his grasp on her butt. Heat pooled beneath her belly, and she was blissfully aware of his erection pushing against the juncture of her thighs.

They made out like that for a few minutes more. Like teenagers. Like equals. Like lovers.

But even Buck's addictive embrace was no match for the fatigue claiming her. He chuckled against her swollen lips when a yawn caught her unawares. "Sorry."

She rode the deep, life-affirming laughter that bounced her atop his chest, and she ended up joining him.

"Believe me. You've got nothing to apologize for." He planted one last, firm, possessive kiss on her mouth before easing his grip on her hair and bottom. Then he tucked her head beneath his chin and hugged her close, anchoring her on top of him. "Sleep, sweetheart. We'll finish this another time."

She was vaguely aware of Jelly climbing onto her shelf above the bed, joining the rest of the troop who was circling around her, embracing her. "Jelly let you pick her up tonight. Guess I'm not the only one who knows how good it feels to be held by you."

"You did good tonight, Chels," Buck whispered against her hair. "I'm so proud of you. But even more than gettin' the bad guy, I need you to be safe, love. I need you to put yourself first for a little while."

Love? Had Buck used the word *love*? Maybe she was already asleep and dreaming.

Chelsea's weary brain was still fritzing with fear,

stress and the dissipating adrenaline rush of finally putting a real name to her tormentor and stopping the manipulation of the crime lab's databases. She couldn't be sure of anything at that moment as physical and emotional fatigue dragged her down toward the oblivion of slumber. Cocooned by Buck's arms and body, she turned her head to breathe in his calming, consuming scent. She felt safe in this man's arms. She felt like she finally had a home.

"I love you," she whispered against his skin.

Maybe that was part of the dream, too.

WAKING UP IN Buck's arms had given Chelsea the positive mindset to get a lot accomplished before Buck dropped her off at Sin City to work the Saturday night reopening with Vinnie. Even though she'd had a mini-breakdown and had wakened to the news that TJ Hawthorne had gotten away before KCPD could get to his house and arrest him, she'd had the best sleep of her life. Not for one moment had she flashed back to her foster father coming into her bedroom, or Dennis making her life a living hell at work, or *Trouble* haunting her nightmares with his threats. Even mentally and emotionally exhausted, she'd innately known that she was safe. She even suspected she was loved. For a woman who'd been alone for as long as she had, finding that connection, that desire, that utter trust in a man's arms was heady stuff.

One reason she'd turned to hacking was because she wanted someone to connect with in the middle of the night when the nightmares and insecurity were more than she could handle on her own. Her pets and counseling had gone a long way to help. Her friends at the crime lab had filled an emotional void, given her a sense of family. But she'd never thought she could fall in love.

And then she'd met Buck.

Her instincts had told her from their first meeting that Robert "Buck" Buckner was a man she could trust. A man who would stand between her and the dangers of the world. A man who would work beside her to make that world a better place. They were certainly an unexpected couple—but she couldn't imagine herself being with anyone else.

The time had come to repay Buck for his protection and kindness and acceptance. For all those breakfasts. All those hugs. All those late-night texts. For those hot arms and that silly Scottish brogue and the way that man could kiss.

The time had come to keep the promise she'd made to Buck. To keep the promise she'd made to herself.

The time had come to make Buck smile.

She carried a whiskey and a sparkling water to the two men seated in the first booth, and offered them both a smile before she tucked the tray beneath her arm and pulled out her phone to read Buck's latest text.

Hawthorne's in the wind. Motorcycle missing. The department has an APB out on him. But this guy is good at staying in the shadows. I was there when the detectives talked to his mother and father. They've got no clue where he is. That's a contentious relationship. They've spent a lot of money on him and want him to finish school or get a job.

Chelsea rolled her eyes and typed her response. He

has a job. It's just that running scams and interfering with police investigations is illegal.

Smart-ass. ;) He hasn't shown up at Sin City, has he?

No. No hooker in the corner.

Double smart-ass. ;) Vinnie's there with you?

   Of course. It's the Saturday night regulars. Gordy and his biker buddies. Martin. She hesitated to add the next words. A couple of newbies.

They're all minding their manners?

Yes.

Trouble hasn't sent you any more threats?

No. I've got my laptop set up to monitor if he gets online anywhere. I'll call you ASAP if I get a lead on his location.

You're staying inside?

Yes. I'm safe. When will you be here?

On my way.

Good. I have a surprise for you.

Killin' me here, sweetheart. I do NOT like surprises at Sin City.

Just hurry. I miss you.

Stay safe.

You, too.

Ten minutes later, Buck opened the door to Sin City and strode straight over to the bar where Chelsea was washing glasses. He eyeballed Gordy Bismarck and his buddies who whistled and shouted taunts about the cop walking into their bar. He exchanged a salute with Vinnie who was pouring beers from the tap, and patted Martin's shoulder in greeting. She quickly dried her hands and hurried around the bar to catch him in a hug before he recognized the guy with the black-haired man bun sitting on the stool beside Martin.

But she was too late.

"What the hell? Kendrick?" Buck's long wool coat was cold against her cheek from the chilly air outside, but she slipped her arms inside to be snugged against his abundant warmth. The welcome was short-lived, though, as Buck shifted her to his side, keeping his arm around her shoulders. "He giving you a hard time?"

"I'm fine." She tried to extricate herself from his protective stance. "I contacted Art tonight, while you and Rufus were helping with the manhunt for TJ. He answered some questions for me."

"Mr. Buckner." The temperamental chef got up from his stool and extended a hand that Buck refused to take. Art pulled his hand back and tucked his fingers into the front pockets of his jeans, nodding as if he'd expected the rejection. "I want you to understand—

I'm not always that big of an ass, but I was protecting someone I care about."

"What are you talking about?" Buck glared at Art before she could explain. "That's why you were rude to Chelsea at the shelter? Why you wouldn't answer my questions? And now you've cornered her here when she's on her own?" His gaze dropped to Chelsea for an explanation. "Did I miss a text that said you needed me?"

"I invited him here. Art, and his partner." She tilted her gaze up to his, unable to contain her smile. "Buck. I'm good at what I do."

He took her by the shoulders and turned away from Art. "I know that, sweetheart. You identified *Trouble*. Once we catch him, he's going to jail. You're going to get all the cases at the crime lab back on track." He nodded back to Art. "I still don't know why that hot-head is here."

She reached up and cradled Buck's stubbled jaw and turned him to look her in the eyes. "No. I'm *really* good. I turned TJ's *Murder Eraser* and *Identity Eraser* websites over to a federal investigator today. Froze his assets. I've already tracked down some of the people who hired him to manipulate their digital footprint, and sent that information over to the cold case squad."

"That's great. I'm sure that won't make Hawthorne very happy. But KCPD is lucky to have you on their side."

He was too on guard against Art Kendrick to get the significance of what she was saying. "So are you."

"I know that, sweetheart."

A cheer went up from the men and women gathered

around the dart games, and a large man separated himself from the group and strode toward the bar.

"I want a rematch, newbie!" Gordy shouted above the cheers and jeers.

But the big man waved him off. When he reached the bar, Art took the man's empty glass and set it on top. The two men exchanged a curious look before Art reached up to squeeze the big man's arm.

"Buck." Chelsea cupped the sides of Buck's jaw between both hands now. She gazed up at him with all the love in her heart and took a deep breath. Then she stretched up on tiptoe and pressed a kiss to his forehead before turning him around to face the blond man beside Art. "I'd like you to meet Clark Remington."

Chelsea watched the blood drain from Buck's face before his cheeks reddened and he pulled the young man into a tight embrace. "Bobby?"

Tears welled up in Chelsea's eyes and spilled over as Buck's son grabbed a fistful of Buck's coat and matched the strength of his father's hug. Art's hand splayed in the middle of Bobby's back, and Chelsea mirrored his stance with Buck as both big men held each other and cried for a few minutes.

"My God, son. Are you all right? You healthy? Clean? Safe?"

"All of the above."

"What happened? Why did you leave us? You know I thought the worst. Why didn't you let me help?"

Bobby eased his grip on Buck's coat and pulled back enough to look his father in the eyes. "It's Clark now. Got myself in trouble and needed to hide. Because I knew you *would* help. Even if it wrecked your career with KCPD or put you in an impossible situation where you'd have to arrest me. But Chelsea says you're not a cop anymore. And that she can find and erase the video I was being blackmailed with. I was with a guy and, well, I didn't know it was being taped and distributed. So, I disappeared. Lived on the streets for a few months until I scraped up enough money to change my identity. Then Tess took me in at the shelter. She doesn't know anything about my past—she took me in. Put me to work. I've stayed clean, found a purpose, grown up—I'm good."

"Are you safe now? Are you still being blackmailed? Can you be prosecuted?"

Clark's whiskey-brown eyes darted past his father to Chelsea. "Chelsea seems to think the law would see me as the victim, not a criminal."

"I'm not a hundred percent sure," Chelsea added. "I told him a little about my experience with sexual assault and exploitation of a minor. I gave his name to Kenna Parker-Watson at the DA's office. She's looking into it."

Buck swiped the tears from his face, capturing his son's face between his hands and studying every change in his countenance. "Bobby? Er, Clark? That'll take some getting used to."

The younger man chuckled, and the sound danced on a low pitch, just like Buck's laugh. "Yeah, Dad. It's me. Don't you have anything else to say? Want to ground me for running away? Have a heart-to-heart? Yell?"

Buck pulled him in for one more back-slapping hug before releasing him. He sank onto the barstool behind him, as if he was too overcome to stand. "Hell, son. I only wanted to see with my own eyes that you were all right. I refused to believe you were dead, but I knew you were in trouble, and it killed me that I couldn't keep you safe."

"I know Dad. I'm so sorry. I handled things the best way I knew how as a teenager. Maybe not the smartest way. But what's done is done. I've been living with my choices ever since."

Chelsea drifted back a step and dabbed at her own tears. Other than Clark's dyed hair and the number of interesting lines missing from his young face, the two men could be twins.

"Your disappearance broke your mother's heart. She couldn't deal."

Clark sank onto the stool beside Buck. "Chelsea told me. I'm so sorry about the divorce. I didn't mean—"

"You had nothing to do with that. You just gave her a reason to walk away from a marriage that wasn't working. I think she's happy, though. Except for missing you."

"I've been trying to atone for my mistakes. Help others out. Protect those who can't protect themselves, like you always did." Clark held out his hand to the man she could now easily see was his boyfriend. "That's how Art and I met. Leaving the Warriors wasn't an easy thing. He'd had the hell beat out of him when I found him, took him in."

Art nodded. "He saved my life. I'm sorry, sir. But if Clark said he didn't want his father to know he was still alive, I wasn't going to tell you. I owe him everything."

"Still think you need an attitude adjustment. But I can appreciate loyalty like that. Especially to this guy." Buck couldn't seem to stop touching his son. He squeezed his shoulder. "Look at you. I knew you were getting taller, but you've bulked up."

"Kind of necessary for the unofficial bodyguard kind of work I've been doing around No-Man's Land."

"That's all legal?" Buck asked.

"Yeah. It's how I earn my keep with Tess and the folks around the shelter."

"Gerald Vaughn?"

"He got mugged by some other homeless guys. I stopped them."

"Brandy Tolliver?"

"She's working her butt off to make a better life for herself. I figure it's the least we could do to keep her safe while she's doing it."

"You need to call your mother."

"I will."

Buck finally released him. "You going to disappear again?"

Clark exchanged a look with Art, then shrugged. "I kind of like what I'm doing now. But… I miss you. So, I'm probably not coming home. But if Chelsea and the DA's office can clear my name, I wouldn't mind coming over for a visit. And a road trip out to Colorado to see Mom."

Buck snapped his fingers at a sudden idea, then pulled a business card from his jacket pocket. "If you're already doing protection work, I could offer you a job at my security firm."

Clark chuckled. "Baby steps, Dad. If I can clear a background check and get a high school transcript, I'd like to go back to school at least part-time to finish my degree."

"I can help with that," Chelsea offered.

"I can get you any references you need," Buck assured him. "I've got some connections at Williams University I can call on, too."

"Like I said, baby steps, Dad. I've been keeping a low profile for so long, it'll take me a while to reintegrate into regular society."

Buck nodded, then extended his arm toward Art. This time, the two men shook hands. "You're the new guy, huh? I take it you're nicer to my son than you are to the folks in your kitchen."

"Dad…" Clark warned.

"Promise you won't disappear without a trace again. Talk to me. Let me help if I can. At the very least, let me know you're okay."

"I will."

"In case you change your mind. And so you always have a way to contact me. Either of you." Buck tucked the card into the pocket of Clark's shirt and handed a second one to Art. Then he stood and turned to Vinnie, who seemed to be wiping some tears of his own with the sleeve of his shirt. Buck twirled his finger in the air, indicating the whole bar. "Drinks are on me."

Vinnie grinned and went to work. "Now you're talking."

Clark and Art stepped up to the bar as Buck pulled Chelsea aside. "You did it. Rufus said if anyone could find Bobby, you could. If there was any trace of him anywhere online, you'd find him. You. Are. A. Miracle. Worker. Thank you." Then he dipped his head, framed her face between his warm, calloused hands and gave her one of *those* kisses. Thorough. A little wild. Demanding and far too brief before he pulled away. He wiped the tears from her cheeks with the pads of his thumbs and looked into her eyes with such intensity that Chelsea's insides clenched with lusty anticipation. Her fingers wrapped around his wrists, for balance, for warmth, because she loved him. "I owe you everything."

"I'll settle for breakfast."

Robert Buckner had strong, straight white teeth, and she saw nearly every one of them as he smiled. "It's a date."

"Ladybug," Vinnie interrupted, shoving a tray of drinks across the bar. "Get these over to Gordy and his boys."

Buck shrugged out of his coat and reached for the tray. "Let me."

"I got it." She lifted the heavy tray before smiling up at Buck and tilting her head toward Clark, née Bobby. "You do the manly bonding thing with your son. I can handle Gordy."

Buck slapped his arm around Clark's shoulders and ordered a coffee while Chelsea moved toward the high tables by the dartboards.

She'd only taken a few steps when the front door shattered with a hail of bullets.

Very real bullets.

The tray teetered out of her hands as the glasses exploded. Something hot snaked across her upper arm and she dove for the floor, even as Buck's familiar weight landed on top of her.

TJ Hawthorne looked like a wild, unkempt man who lived on the street as he burst into the bar. "You stupid bitch! You think you can take me down? You know what people are going to do to me if I don't come through for them? I've got a reputation to maintain." What kind of reputation did a spoiled twenty-four-year-old college failure with delusions of grandeur have to maintain? "I'm done playing games. Now you'll have to die—!"

Several things happened all at once. Buck swore at the blood pooling on the floor beneath her. A dozen other weapons slipped from holsters and cocked in the air behind her. "Drop your weapons!" Keeping his body between her and TJ, Buck pulled his gun and turned to fire.

But Clark had TJ in a headlock and was taking him down to the floor.

"Stay down," Buck ordered against her ear, and then he was on his feet, securing TJ's weapon and helping his son subdue the desperate young man. Once TJ's arms were bound with his own belt behind his back, Buck stood and pointed to the bikers behind Chelsea. "I said to put those guns away."

Art and Vinnie had come out from behind the bar to roll Chelsea over and press a towel to the wound on her arm while Buck was on his phone, calling Rufus for backup. She lived in a strange world where a biker gang had an ex-cop's back. "Nobody shoots up our bar," Gordy announced, motioning for his buddies to return their weapons to their hidden holsters. "Especially some namby-pamby college boy. There better not be any bullet holes or ricochets on our bikes."

Buck barely looked up as he cupped Chelsea's face and probed her for injuries beyond the graze along her upper arm. "Why don't you boys go check out the parking lot. I got this."

Twenty minutes later, Rufus King had arrested TJ and loaded him into the back of his squad car. Gordy and the Missouri Twisters Motorcycle Club declared they were heading out before any more cops arrived. Bobby and Art had headed back to the Yankee Hill Shelter with the promise to keep in touch.

Despite her protests, Buck picked up Chelsea and carried her to a barstool, where he peeled off her sweater to examine the bullet graze on her upper arm. "Vinnie. You got that first aid kit and a clean towel?"

Chelsea grinned from ear to ear, even though her upper arm was throbbing. "Two challenges down. We found Bobby and took down *Trouble*. All that's left is to testify against Dennis, and then I can have my happily-ever-after." She adjusted her glasses on the bridge of her nose and worried at the intense look in Buck's whiskey-brown eyes. "You're part of that happily-ever-after, I hope."

"Damn right I am." He paused a moment to press a kiss to her forehead before tying off the makeshift bandage around her arm. "I'm taking you to the ER."

Enough. She threw her arms around Buck's neck, knocking him back a step. But he caught her squarely against his chest and claimed her mouth as thoroughly as she was claiming his.

"You are going to be the death of me, woman." He pulled back, smiling down at her. "But I have a feeling I'm going to die a very happy man."

* * * * *

Look for K-9 Patrol, *the first book in*
USA TODAY *bestselling author Julie Miller's*
Kansas City Crime Lab miniseries, available now.
And you'll find more books in the series coming
soon, wherever Harlequin Intrigue books are sold!

#2115 LAWMAN TO THE CORE
The Law in Lubbock County • by Delores Fossen

When an intruder attacks Hallie Stanton and tries to kidnap the baby she's adopting, her former boss, ATF agent Nick Brodie, is on the case. But will his feelings for Hallie and her son hinder his ability to shut down a dangerous black market baby ring?

#2116 DOCKSIDE DANGER
The Lost Girls • by Carol Ericson

To protect his latest discovery, FBI agent Tim Ruskin needs LAPD homicide detective Jane Falco off the case. But when intel from the FBI brass clashes with the clues Jane is uncovering, Tim's instincts tell him to put his trust in the determined cop, peril be damned.

#2117 MOUNTAIN TERROR
Eagle Mountain Search and Rescue • by Cindi Myers

A series of bombings have rocked Eagle Mountain, and Deni Traynor's missing father may be the culprit. SAR volunteer Ryan Welch will help the vulnerable schoolteacher unearth the truth. But will the partnership lead them to their target...or something more sinister?

#2118 BRICKELL AVENUE AMBUSH
South Beach Security • by Caridad Piñeiro

Mariela Hernandez has a target on her back, thanks to her abusive ex-husband's latest plot. Teaming up with Ricky Gonzalez and his family's private security firm is her only chance at survival. With bullets flying, Ricky will risk it all to be the hero Mariela needs.

#2119 DARK WATER DISAPPEARANCE
West Investigations • by K.D. Richards

Detective Terrence Sutton is desperate to locate his missing sister—one of three women who recently disappeared from Carling Lake. The only connection to the crimes? A run-down mansion and Nikki King, the woman Terrence loved years ago and who's now back in town...

#2120 WHAT IS HIDDEN
by Janice Kay Johnson

Jo Summerlin's job at her stepfather's spectacular limestone cavern is thrown into chaos when she and former navy SEAL Alan Burke discover a pile of bones and a screaming stranger. Have they infiltrated a serial killer's perfect hiding place?

HARLEQUIN
PLUS

Announcing a **BRAND-NEW**
multimedia subscription service
for romance fans like you!

Read, Watch and Play.

Experience the easiest way to get
the romance content you crave.

Start your **FREE 7 DAY TRIAL** at
<u>www.harlequinplus.com/freetrial</u>.